Jerry Bauer

About the Author

JEAN-PIERRE VERNANT is a professor at the Collège de France in Paris and one of the foremost classicists of our time. He is the author of numerous scholarly books on Greek thought, myths, tragedy, politics, society, and religion.

LINDA ASHER, a former editor at *The New Yorker*, has translated many French language writers into English, including Restif de la Bretonne, Victor Hugo, George Simenon, and Milan Kundera.

The Universe, the
Gods, and Men

The Universe, the Gods, and Men

Ancient Greek Myths

Told by
Jean-Pierre Vernant

Translated from the French
by Linda Asher

Perennial

An Imprint of HarperCollins*Publishers*

This work is published with the assistance of the French Ministry of Culture, National Center for Books.

This book was first published in France in 1999 by Éditions du Seuil.

A hardcover edition of this book was published in 2001 by HarperCollins Publishers.

First Perennial edition published 2002.

Designed by The Book Design Group

The Library of Congress has catalogued the hardcover edition as follows:
Vernant, Jean-Pierre.
    [L'univers, les dieux, les hommes. English]
    The universe, the gods, and men : ancient Greek myths;
    translated from the French by Linda Asher.
        p. cm.
    ISBN 0-06-019775-7
    1. Mythology, Greek. I. Asher, Linda. II. Title.
BL782.V4613 2001
292.1'3—dc21   2001016844

ISBN 0-06-095750-6 (pbk.)

02 03 04 05 06 ❖/RRD 10 9 8 7 6 5 4 3 2 1

Contents

Author's Preface

Once upon a Time . . . was the title I first thought to give this book. In the end I decided to replace it with something more explicit. But here, on the threshold of the work, I cannot help mentioning the memory that echoed in that original title, and that gave rise to these pages.

A quarter century ago, when my grandson was a child and spent his vacations with my wife and me, one routine came to be as imperative as bathing and meals: Every evening, when the time came for Julien to go to bed, I would hear him call to me from his room, often rather impatiently: "J.-P.—the story! The story!" I would go sit beside him and tell him some Greek legend. It was no trouble for me to pull something out of the repertory of myths that I spent my professional time analyzing, dissecting, comparing, and interpreting as I worked to understand them, but that I passed along to him in another way—straight out, however they came to me, like a fairy tale. My only concern was to follow the thread of the story from start to finish holding on to its dramatic tension: "Once upon a time . . ." Julien was all ears, and looked happy. I was, too. I took delight in passing on to him straight from my mouth to his ear a little of that Greek universe for which I care so much, and whose survival in each of us seems to me more necessary than ever in today's world. It also pleased me that this heritage should come to him orally, like what Plato calls "nursery tales"—like other things that travel from one generation to the next quite apart from any official teaching, without passing through books, and that form an unwritten stock of knowledge and practices: everything from rules of propriety in speech and action, of right behavior, to physical techniques—styles of walking, running, swimming, biking, climbing . . .

Of course it was quite naive to think I was helping to keep alive a tradition of ancient legends by putting my voice to work every evening reciting them to a child. But it was a period, you may recall—I'm speaking of the seventies—when myth was in full sail. After the work of Georges Dumézil and Claude Lévi-Strauss, the fever for mythology studies had recruited a little band of Hellenists, and we all plunged into exploring the legendary world of ancient Greece. As we made our way into it and our analyses progressed, the existence of a general style of mythic thought came to seem more problematic, and we were led to inquire, "What is a myth?" Or more specifically, given our area of research, "What is a Greek myth?" A story, yes of course. But the question remains how these stories are formed, established, transmitted, preserved. Now, in the case of the Greek myths, they only reach us late in their career, as written texts, the oldest of which belong to all literary genres—epic, poetry, tragedy, history, even philosophy. And even there the myths most often occur in fragments, scattered, sometimes only by allusion, except in *The Iliad*, *The Odyssey*, and Hesiod's *Theogony*. It was very recently—only toward the start of our own time—that scholars collected those many and fairly divergent traditions and put them together in a single corpus, set one after another as if on the shelves of a *Library* (to use the title Apollodorus actually gave his own collection, which became a great classic in the field). Thus was built what we have come to call Greek mythology.

Myth, mythology—these are of course Greek words, linked to the history and to certain features of that civilization. Should we therefore conclude that the terms have no pertinence outside that civilization—that myth and mythology exist only in the Greek form and in the Greek sense? Quite the contrary: To be understood themselves, the Hellenic legends must be compared to the traditional stories of other peoples from very diverse cultures and periods, whether ancient China, India, the Middle East, the Pre-Columbian Americas, or Africa. The comparison is necessary because those narrative traditions, however they differ, display enough common elements, both with one another and with the Greek example, to establish kinship among them. Lévi-Strauss can declare it as indisputable observation that no matter where it comes from, a myth is instantly recognizable as such with no risk of confusion with other kinds of story. It bears a marked distinction from the historical story, which in Greece grew up somewhat in contrast to myth, insofar as it was meant to be the accurate account of events recent enough to be confirmed by trustworthy witnesses. As for the literary story, it is pure fiction presented frankly as such, whose value derives primarily from the talent and skill of the person who made it. These two types of story are normally attributed to an author, who answers for them and who offers them under his name, as written texts, to an audience of readers.

The status of the myth is another thing entirely. It occurs as a story from ancient times that already existed before any particular storyteller undertook to tell it. In that sense the myth-story arises from neither personal invention nor creative fancy but rather from transmission and memory. This intimate and functional connection with memorization brings myth near to poetry, which originally—in its earliest manifestations—looks much like the process of mythic elaboration. The Homeric epic is an example: To weave its stories about the adventures of legendary heroes, the epic operates primarily in the mode of oral poetry, composed and sung before its audience by successive generations of bards inspired by the goddess of memory, Mnemosine; only later does it undergo formal drafting, whose purpose is to establish and fix the official text.

Even in our time too, a poem exists only when it is spoken; it needs to be learned by heart and, to bring it to life, recited with the silent words of interior speech. Myth too is only alive when it goes on being recounted, from generation to generation, in the course of daily existence. Otherwise, relegated to the depths of libraries, congealed into written forms, it turns into a scholarly reference for an elite of readers who specialize in mythology.

Memory, orality, tradition: These are the very conditions of myth's existence and survival. They impose on it certain characteristics, which emerge more clearly if we extend the comparison between poetical activity and myth activity. The differing role of speech in the two activities clarifies an essential difference. Since the time of the troubadours, when poetry in the West became autonomous—when it drew apart not only from the great mythic stories but also from the music that had accompanied it up until the fourteenth century—it has become a specific domain of linguistic expression. From that time on, every poem stands as a unique construction—very complex, certainly polysemous—but so strictly organized, so interconnected among its various sections and at all its levels, that it must be memorized and recited exactly as it is, with no omission or change whatever. The poem remains identical throughout every performance of it, wherever and whenever it occurs. The utterance that brings the poetic text to life, in public for listeners or in private for oneself, has a single unchanging face. One word varied, one line skipped, one rhythm dislocated, and the whole edifice of the poem lies shattered.

The myth-story, on the other hand, is both polysemous like a poetic text, in its multiple layers of meaning; and, unlike a poem, not fixed in a definitive form. It always contains variants, many versions available to the storyteller, from which he selects according to the circumstances of the audience or of his own preferences, and which he can strike out, add to, or change as he likes. For as long as an oral-legend tradition is vital, as long as it stays in touch with the outlooks and customs of a group, it keeps changing: the story remains somewhat open to innovation. When the researcher in ancient myth comes upon it late in the game, already fossilized in literary or scholarly texts as I said about the Greek situation, then to decode it correctly each legend requires him to broaden his explorations stage by stage: first from one version to all the others, however minor, on the same theme; then to other myth-stories near or remote and even to texts from other sectors of that same culture—literary, scientific, political, philosophical; and ultimately, to more or less similar narratives from distant civilizations. What actually interests the historian and the anthropologist is the intellectual background indicated by the narrative line—the loom it's woven on—which can only be discerned by comparing the stories, in the play of their differences and resemblances. In fact, the various mythologies might all be described by Jacques Roubaud's very apt remarks on the Homeric poems, with their legendary element: "They are not merely stories. They contain the treasury of ideas, linguistic forms, cosmological imaginings, moral precepts, and so on, that make up the common heritage of the Greeks in the preclassical era."*

The investigator digging away to unearth these underlying "treasures," this common Greek heritage, may sometimes feel frustrated, as if in the course of the search he had lost sight of the "enormous pleasure" La Fontaine foresaw for anyone hearing the story "Peau d'âne." That pleasure in the story, which I mentioned at the beginning of this preface, I would have relinquished without much regret except that a quarter century ago, on that same lovely island where I shared vacations and stories with Julien, some friends one day asked me to tell them some Greek myths. Which I did. They made me promise—they were insistent enough to persuade me—to write down what I had narrated to them. It wasn't easy. The move from spoken word to written text is very difficult. Not only because writing lacks the things that give flesh and life to the oral tale—voice, tone, rhythm, gesture—but also because the two forms of expression derive from two different kinds of thought. When an oral presentation is reproduced on paper as is, the text doesn't hold up. And when, conversely, the text is first created in writing, reading it aloud fools no one: It is not made to be heard by listeners; it stands outside the oral. That initial problem—to write as one speaks—is compounded by several others. First of all the writer must choose one version—that is, ignore the variants, erase them, silence them. And in the very way he or she recounts the chosen version, the narrator intrudes personally and takes on the role of interpreter, precisely because no definitive model yet exists for the myth-scenario that is being set out. And furthermore, how could the researcher ignore the

* Jacques Roubaud, Poésie, Mémoire, Lecture (Paris–Tübingen–Esslingen: Editions Isele, Collection "Les Conférences du Divan," 1998), p. 10.

fact, when he turns storyteller, that he is also a scholar seeking to understand the intellectual underpinnings of the myths, and that he is going to inject into his tale those meanings his earlier studies have led him to consider important?

I was quite aware of those obstacles and those dangers. Nonetheless I took the plunge. I have tried to do the telling as if the tradition of those myths could still be kept going. The voice that for centuries spoke directly to the Greek audience and that has since fallen silent—I hoped it could be heard again by the readers of today; I hoped that here and there in certain pages of this book, if I've succeeded, the echo of that voice would still resonate.

The Universe, the
Gods, and Men

The Origin of the Universe

What was there when there was not yet anything, when there was nothing? The Greeks answered that question with stories and myths.

At the very beginning, what existed first was the Void; the Greeks say Chaos. What is the Void? It is an emptiness, a dark emptiness where nothing is visible. A realm of falling, of vertigo and confusion—endless, bottomless. That Void seizes us like the yawning of an immense gullet where everything is swallowed up by murky darkness. So at the start there is only that Void, a blind, black, boundless abyss.

Then Earth appears. The Greeks call it Gaia. Earth rises up in the very heart of the Void. And here it is: born after Chaos, and in some respects its opposite. Earth is not that realm of falling, dark

and boundless and undefined; Earth has a distinct, separate, precise form. Against the confusion and shadowy vagueness of Chaos
stand Gaia's sharpness, firmness, stability. On Earth everything is
outlined, visible, solid. Gaia can be defined as the entity upon
which the gods, men, and beasts can walk with confidence. It is
the floor of the world.

THE DEPTHS OF THE EARTH: THE VOID

The world now has a floor, born out of the vast Void. At one end
this floor rises upward as mountains; at the other it plunges downward as underground. That nether-earth stretches on forever,
unbounded—so that, in a way, what underlies Gaia, beneath the
firm and solid ground, is still the abyss, Chaos. Earth arose out of
the heart of the Void but still clings to it deep down. To the Greek
mind this Chaos evokes a kind of impenetrable murk in which all
frontiers are scrambled. At the bottommost reach of Earth there is
still that original chaotic element.

Though Earth is quite visible, though it has a clear-cut form,
and though anything born of the Earth may possess those same
distinct edges and boundaries—yet, in its depths, Earth remains
akin to the Void. It is a Black Earth. The adjectives that describe
Earth in the stories can be much like those that describe the Void.
The Black Earth stretches between the low and the high; between
on the one hand the darkness and the rootedness in the Void that
its deep places embody, and on the other, the snowcapped mountains that Earth thrusts toward the sky, the shining mountains
whose highest pinnacles reach up into that realm of the sky continually drenched in light.

In the house that is the cosmos, the Earth constitutes the foundation, but that is not its only function. It breeds and nourishes everything, except for certain entities, to be discussed later, that come from Chaos. Gaia is the universal mother: Forests, mountains, underground caves, ocean waters, vast sky—all of them come from Gaia, Mother Earth. So first there was the abyss, the Void, an enormous gullet in the form of a lightless, boundless chasm; but later that Void gives onto a solid floor—the Earth—the Earth that leaps to the heights, descends to the depths.

After Chaos and Earth, third in the sequence comes what the Greeks called Eros and later called "Old Love" (pictures show him with white hair): This is primordial Love. Why this primordial Eros? Because back in those distant times, there was no masculine or feminine yet, no sexed or gendered beings. This original Eros is not the one who will appear later on, with the occurrence of men and women, males and females. From that point on, the problem will be to pair off opposite sexes, which necessarily calls for some desire on the part of each, some kind of consent.

So *Chaos* is a neuter term, not masculine. *Gaia*, Mother Earth, is obviously a feminine term. But whom can she love outside herself, since she is all alone with only Chaos? Eros, after Void and Earth the third entity to appear, is not the same figure who later presides over gendered lovemaking. The original Eros expresses a new thrust in the universe: In the same way that Earth emerged from Void, from out of Earth there springs what she contains within her own depths. What was in her, as part of her essence, comes forth and out: She gives birth to it with no need for sexual congress with anyone. What Earth delivers and reveals is precisely the thing that had dwelled darkly within her.

Earth first gives birth to a very important figure, Uranus—Sky, and Starry Sky at that. Next she is delivered of Pontus, water—all waters, and specifically those of the sea. And Earth conceived them without coupling with any other being. Through her own internal power, Earth develops an entity that already lay within her and that, the moment she expels it, becomes her double and her opposite. She produces Starry Sky equal to herself—a replica just as solid, as substantial, and the same size as she is. Uranus then stretches out on her. Earth and Sky are two superimposed planes of the universe—a floor and a ceiling, a bottom and a top—and they cover each other completely.

Earth gives birth to Pontus, or Sea, and he thereupon completes her and insinuates himself inside her—he sets her boundaries with his vast liquid expanses. Like Uranus, Sea also represents the opposite of Earth: Earth is solid, compact, nonporous—things cannot blend into it—whereas Sea is all liquidness, shapeless ungraspable fluidity: His waters mingle, undifferentiated and flowing together. Sea is bright at the surface, but in his deep reaches it is utterly dark—and this links him, like Earth, to a chaotic strain.

Thus the world is constructed out of three primordial entities: Chaos, Gaia, Eros, plus two offspring of Earth: Uranus and Pontus—Sky and Sea. All of them are natural powers and divinities at the same time: Gaia is both the earth we walk on and a goddess; Sea represents the waters and is also a divine power that can be worshiped. Thereby hang tales of another sort—violent, dramatic stories.

THE CASTRATION OF URANUS

Let us start with Sky, or Uranus: born of Gaia, and the same dimension as she. He lies sprawled upon her who brought him into being. Sky covers Earth totally; every segment of earth is matched by a patch of sky stuck tight to her. From the moment that Gaia—the powerful divinity, Mother Earth—produces Uranus, her exact correspondent, her duplicate, her symmetrical double, we are in the presence of a pair of opposites: a male and a female. Uranus is *the* Male Sky just as Gaia is *the* Female Earth. Now that Uranus is in the picture, Love plays out differently. It is no longer just Gaia producing what she contains inside herself, or Uranus what he has inside himself; now creatures different from both of them issue from the joining of these two powers.

Uranus never stops pouring his seed into Gaia's loins. The primordial Uranus has no activity other than sex. Covering Gaia ceaselessly, as much as he can—that is his sole idea and all he does. So poor Earth is constantly pregnant with a whole stream of children—who cannot get out of her belly, who stay stuck right where Uranus begat them. Since Sky never pulls apart from Earth, there is no space between them to let their offspring—the Titans—emerge into the light and live an autonomous existence. They cannot take on their own shape, they cannot become individualized beings, because they are endlessly thrust back into Gaia's loins just as Uranus himself was contained in Gaia's loins before he was born.

Who are the children of Gaia and Uranus? To begin with, there are six Titans and their six Titan sisters. The first of the Titans is named Oceanus. He is that liquid belt that rings the universe and flows in a circle, so that he ends where he begins; the cosmic river turns on itself in a closed circuit. The youngest Titan is named Cronus; he is known as "Treacherous-Minded Cronus." Aside from the Titan brothers and sisters, Gaia and Uranus also produce two sets of hugely monstrous beings. The first set is the three Cyclops giants—Brontes, Steropes, and Arges—very powerful figures with only one eye each, and names that give some sense of the sort of metalwork they do: the rumble of thunder, the explosive flash of lightning. It is they, in fact, who craft the thunderbolt as a gift for Zeus. A second trio is made up of the beings called Hecatonchires—the Hundred-Armed Creatures: Cottus, Briareus, Gyes. These are monsters of enormous size, each with fifty heads and a hundred arms, and each arm endowed with a terrible power.

Alongside the Titans—those first deities to have individual characteristics (unlike Gaia, Uranus, or Pontus, who are only names for natural forces)—the three Cyclopes represent the blaze of sight. Each has a single eye in the center of the forehead, but that eye has a blasting force, like the weapon they present to Zeus. The magical power of the eye. As to the Hundred-Armed Creatures, their brute force represents the ability to conquer—to win by pure physical arm power. So from the one squad, the force of a blasting eye, and from the other the force of a hand that can bind up, crush, break, conquer, and rule over every creature in the world. Meanwhile, though, Titans and Hundred-Armed Creatures and Cyclopes are all still caught inside Gaia's belly; Uranus is still sprawling over her.

There is really no light as yet because Uranus maintains an endless night by lying on Gaia. Then Earth lets loose her resentment. She is furious that her children are still inside her; with no space to emerge into, they are swelling her to bursting, packing her, choking her. She calls on them—on the Titans in particular— saying, "Listen here! Your father, Sky, is doing us all injury, he is inflicting dreadful violence on us, this has to end. You must rise up against your father." The Titans inside Gaia's belly are terrified at her forceful words. Uranus is still planted firmly on their mother, just as enormous as she: He does not seem easily undone. Only the last-born son, Cronus, agrees to help Gaia and take his father on.

Earth works out a very wily plan. To carry it out, inside herself she shapes a steely instrument—a sickle, a *harpē*. She puts the sickle handle into young Cronus's fist. He is crouched in his mother's belly right where Uranus penetrates her; he lies in wait there, in ambush. Just as Uranus empties his seed into Gaia, Cronus grasps his father's sexual parts with his left hand, he grips them firmly and, wielding the sickle with his right hand, he slices them off. Then, without looking behind him, to ward off the bad luck his act might bring, he throws Uranus's male organ over his shoulder. From that organ, severed and flung behind him, drops of blood fall to the ground, but the organ itself flies still farther off and into the briny deep. At the instant he is castrated, Uranus utters a howl of pain and pulls abruptly away from Gaia. He goes to settle at the very summit of the world, never to leave it again. And because Uranus is as long and wide as Gaia, there is not a single yard of land anywhere without an equivalent yard of sky located above it.

EARTH, SPACE, SKY

In castrating Uranus, on his mother's advice and through her shrewd tactics, Cronus brings about a fundamental stage in the birth of the cosmos: He separates the earth from the sky. Between sky and earth he creates open space: Everything the earth produces, everything living beings engender, will now have room to breathe, to live. Space is liberated—but time is transformed as well. As long as Uranus weighed heavy on Gaia, there were no generations following one after another; they stayed buried inside the being that had produced them. But the moment Uranus withdraws, the Titans can emerge from the maternal belly and produce offspring themselves. Thus begins a succession of generations. Space has opened up, and the "starry sky" now functions as a ceiling, a kind of great murky platform stretching over the earth. From time to time this dark sky brightens, for henceforth day and night alternate: first comes a dark sky with only the light of the stars, then a bright sky with clouds the only shadow.

Let us quit Earth's family line for a moment, and look at Chaos's brood: This Void produced two offspring, Erebus and Nux, Night. Erebus is the direct continuance of Chaos, utter blackness, the power of blackness in its pure state, nothing admixed whatever. Night, though, is something else again: Like Gaia, she also bears young without any sexual union, as if she'd carved them out of her own dark tissue, and yet those children are Aether—ethereal light—and Hemere, Day—the light of day.

Chaos's child Erebus represents Chaos's characteristic darkness. But his other child, Night, calls Day into being: There is no Night without Day. When Night produces Aether and Hemere, what is she doing? Just as Erebus was darkness in its pure state, Aether is luminosity in its pure state; Aether and Erebus are counterparts. Shining Aether is the region of the sky where there is no darkness ever—the part that belongs to the Olympians. Aether's extraordinarily brilliant light is unstained by any shadow. Night and Day, though, support each other in their very opposition. Now that space has opened up, Night and Day alternate regularly. At the entrance to the netherworld—Tartarus—are the gates of Night that give onto her dwelling place. Night and Day arrive there in turn; they nod, they pass, but they never join or touch. When Night is present, Day is not; when Day is present, Night is not; but without Day there is no Night.

Just as Erebus represents total and utter darkness, so Aether embodies absolute luminosity. All the beings on the earth are creatures who live in day and night both; until death they never experience that total darkness where the sun's rays do not penetrate, Erebus's night. Men, beasts, plants, live both night and day in that juncture of opposites; but the gods, at the pinnacle of heaven, never experience the alternation of day and night; they live in constant brilliance. So: Above are the celestial deities in the shining Aether; and below are the underworld deities, or those who have been conquered and sent into Tartarus, all of them living in a constant night; and then the mortals are here in this world—a world of the two states combined.

Let us return to Uranus. What happens when he takes up his position at the top of the world? He is no longer coupling with Gaia, except during the great rains, when he—Sky—pours out his fecundating fluids and Earth bears offspring. That beneficent rain allows the earth to bring forth new creatures, new plants, grains. But apart from that period, the bond between the earth and the sky is broken.

When Uranus withdrew from Gaia, he cast a terrible curse on his sons: "You will be called Titans," he told them (drawing on the Greek verb *titaino*) "because you *reached* your arms too high; you must pay for the crime of raising your hand against your father." The drops of blood that fell to earth from his severed organ engender the Erinyes—the Furies. These are primitive beings whose essential function is to keep alive the memory of offenses committed by one kinsman against another, and to enforce retribution, however long it takes; they are deities of revenge for crimes against kin. The Erinyes represent hatred, memory—the memory for transgression and the stricture that crime must be avenged.

Along with these Erinyes, or Furies, the blood from Uranus's wound also engendered the Giants and the Meliai, nymphs of the great ash trees. The Giants are essentially soldiers; they personify the violence of war; they have no childhood or old age; their whole life long they are adults in their prime, dedicated to making war, with a taste for murderous battle. The ash-tree nymphs—the Meliai—are warriors as well; they have a strong vocation for slaughter, for the soldiers' battle lances are made of wood from the ash trees the nymphs inhabit. So Uranus's blood breeds three different sorts of creature that incarnate violence, punishment, combat, war, and slaughter. For the Greeks one name summarizes all that violence: It is Eris, which signifies every type and form of conflict, or—in the case of the Erinyes—discord at the heart of a family.

DISCORD AND LOVE

What becomes of that sex organ Cronus threw into the sea? It does not simply sink into the ocean waters; it floats about, it drifts, and its foamy sperm mingles with the foam of the sea. From that foamy mass around the organ, moving to the whim of the waves, arises a splendid creature: Aphrodite, the goddess born of the sea and the foam. She sails for a while and then comes ashore on her island, Cyprus. As she walks on the sand, the most fragrant and beautiful flowers spring up beneath her steps. In Aphrodite's wake, hard on her heels, come Eros and Himeros, love and desire. This is not the original Eros, but a later one who demands that there be masculine and feminine in the world from then on; he is sometimes said to be Aphrodite's son. This Eros has a different task; it is no longer what it was at the very beginning of the cosmos—drawing forth what lay contained in the dark interior of the primordial powers. His job now is to bring together two fully individualized beings, of different genders, in an erotic game predicated on some sexual strategy—with all that that would involve in the way of seduction and accord and jealousy. Eros brings together two different beings to beget a third being, identical to neither parent but perpetuating both. So there is now another sort of creation than in earlier times.

In other words, by cutting off his father's sex organ Cronus gave rise to two powers the Greeks considered complementary: Eris—strife—and Eros—love.

Eris is the struggle within a single family or some other human unit—conflict and discord at the heart of what had been unified. Eros, on the other hand, is agreement and unity between two elements as dissimilar as feminine and masculine can be. Eris and Eros are both produced by the same initiating act that opened space, set time moving, let successive generations step out onto the world's stage—a stage that was now wide open.

Now all these heavenly characters, with Eris on one side and Eros on the other, are going to meet in battle. Why? Less in order to construct the universe whose foundations are already in place than to determine who will rule that universe. Who is to be sovereign? Instead of a cosmogonic tale concerned with such questions as What is the beginning of the world? Why the Abyss first? How did everything in the universe get fabricated? other questions arise, and other stories—far more dramatic ones—seek to answer them. How do the gods, who were themselves created and who created progeny in turn—how do they battle and tear at each other? How do they reach a truce? How are the Titans going to expiate the crime they committed against their father, Uranus; how will they be punished? Who will maintain the stability of this world built out of a nothing that was everything, out of a darkness that was the very source of light, out of an emptiness that begat fullness and solidity? How does the world become stable, ordered, with individualized beings in it? In lifting himself away from Earth, Uranus opens the way to an uninterrupted sequence of generations. But if in each generation the gods go to war again, the world will never have stability. The war of the gods must come to an end so that world order may be definitively established. And the curtain rises on the struggles for divine sovereignty.

The War of the Gods
and Zeus's Kingship

So now the stage is set in the world's theater. Space is open, time progresses, generations will follow one another. There is the subterranean world below; there is the vast earth and the waters and the ocean stream circling it all; and above there is a fixed sky. The earth is a stable base for humans and animals, and high above, the ethereal sky is a similarly secure home for the divinities. The Titans, who are the first gods, properly speaking—the children of Uranus, or Sky—thus have the world at their disposal. They settle high on the mountains of the earth, where the minor divinities also have their permanent homes: the naiads, or water nymphs, the woodland nymphs, and the mountain nymphs—dryads and oreads. Each moves into place for action.

At the very top of the sky are the Titan gods, Uranus's offspring, girls and boys. Their leader is the last-born, the youngest—the cunning, sly, cruel god Cronus. He was the one who unhesitatingly cut off his father's sexual parts. In daring that act, he released the universe, created space, brought about a world that was differentiated and organized. The act was positive, but it had a dark aspect to it: It was also a crime, with a penalty to be paid. For, as Sky retreated to his permanent position, he made sure to lay a curse on his children, the first individualized gods—a curse that did later come into effect under the supervision of the Erinyes, the Furies born from the blood of the mutilation. One day Cronus would have to pay his debt to the Erinyes, his father's avengers.

Thus the youngest but also the boldest of Uranus's sons, the one who carried out Gaia's stratagem for thrusting Sky off and away from her—Cronus—becomes king of the gods and of the world. With him, around him, stand the other Titan gods—lesser, but accessory to the act. Cronus liberated them; they are his protégés.

Two other trios were also born of the embraces of Uranus and Gaia; like their Titan brothers, they too had been trapped in Earth's loins: These are the three Cyclopes and the three Hecatonchires. What's become of them? All signs indicate that Cronus—a jealous, nasty god, ever watchful and alert, worried that some plot is brewing against him—has chained them up. He binds the three Cyclopes and the three Hecatonchires and relegates them to the underworld. But meanwhile the Titans—brothers and sisters—join together in sexual intercourse; notably, Cronus with Rhea. Rhea seems to be a kind of double for Gaia; the two are kindred primordial powers. There is a difference between them, though. Gaia's name is absolutely clear to any Greek—her name is Earth and she *is* the earth—whereas Rhea's is personal, individualized, a name that does not embody a natural element. Rhea represents something more anthropomorphic, more

humanized, more specific, than Gaia. But generally Gaia and Rhea
are like mother and daughter: They are very much alike, they are
alter egos.

IN THE PATERNAL BELLY

Cronus couples with Rhea, and he too begets children who will
bear other children. His offspring constitute a new generation of
divinities, the second generation of individualized gods, with their
names and relationships and realms of influence. But Cronus is
suspicious, jealous, concerned about his power, and he does not
trust his children. He is particularly suspicious now because Gaia
has alerted him. As the mother of all the earliest deities, she is
privy to the secrets of time, she grasps things hidden in its shadowy recesses as they come gradually to light; she knows the future.
Gaia has warned her son that he too may be overthrown by some
child of his—that one of his sons will be stronger than he is, and
will dethrone him. So Cronus's sovereignty is only temporary.
Thoroughly worried, then, Cronus takes some precautions: The
moment a new child is born to him, he eats it up, devours it, puts
it away in his stomach. All the children of Cronus and Rhea are
swallowed down that way, into the paternal belly.

Naturally Rhea is no happier with this behavior than Gaia
was when Uranus kept their children from emerging into the light.
Uranus and Cronus both force their progeny back into the night
of prebirth; they do not wish them to flourish in the light, like any
tree piercing the soil to lead its life between sky and earth. On
Gaia's advice Rhea determines to parry Cronus's outrageous
behavior; she figures out a ruse, a trick, a fraud, a lie. (In so doing,
she is foiling Cronus with the very weapon that defines him, for

he is a god of trickery, a god of lying and duplicity.) When the last of their children, Zeus (the youngest boy, just as Cronus was Uranus's youngest son), is about to be born, Rhea slips off to Crete to deliver in secret. She entrusts the baby to the care of naiads who undertake to raise him deep in a cave so that Cronus suspects nothing, cannot hear the newborn's wailing. Later, as the babe's cries rapidly grow in volume, Rhea asks some male divinities, the Curetes, to station themselves at the mouth of the cave and perform war dances so that the clatter of weapons and other noises and songs will cover the sound of baby Zeus's voice. So Cronus suspects nothing. He did know, though, that Rhea was pregnant, so he expects to see the most recent infant she bore and should soon be showing him. And what does she bring him? A stone. A stone she disguises in an infant's swaddling cloth. She tells Cronus, "Be careful, he's very fragile, he's tiny," and bam! in one gulp, Cronus swallows the swaddled stone. So now all his and Rhea's brood is inside Cronus's belly, with the stone on top of the heap.

Meanwhile, in Crete, Zeus is growing up and growing strong. When he reaches his full maturity, he conceives the idea of making Cronus pay for his crimes against his own children and against Uranus, the father he injured so horribly. How shall he do it? Zeus is alone. He would like to make Cronus disgorge, vomit up, the swarm of children he's got in his belly. And once again it is by cunning that he will manage this—the cunning the Greeks call *metis*—the form of intelligence that works out in advance all sorts of moves to trick the adversary. Zeus's idea is to get Cronus to swallow a *pharmakon*, a drug he'll be told is a magic potion but that is actually an emetic. Rhea serves it to him. No sooner does Cronus swallow it than he starts by vomiting up the stone; then he vomits up the whole string of gods and goddesses in reverse sequence of their birth dates: The youngest follows just after the stone, and the oldest is at the bottom. Thus in his own way—vomiting them up—Cronus repeats the births of all the children Rhea brought into the world.

A FOOD FOR IMMORTALITY

Now a group of gods and goddesses is present to stand with their brother, Zeus. And there begins what may be called the war of the gods—that is, their confrontation in a long struggle that goes unresolved for about ten "long years" (which is to say "many myriads of years": a "long year" can be a hundred or even a thousand years long).

On one side is Cronus, flanked by the other Titan gods; on the other, Zeus, with the figures called the Cronids or Olympians—his siblings, fathered by Cronus, who live on Mount Olympus. Each leader has established his camp atop a mountain, and they battle a long while with victory never tilting clearly one way or the other. The world's theater is now not only established but occupied and torn apart by that endless war between the first-generation gods and the second, their children. Here again cunning will make a difference. There are several skirmishes to this strange battle between divine powers. One thing is certain—victory will go to the camp that can deploy not only brute force but also subtle intelligence. The deciding factors in this indecisive battle are not violence and superior military power but shrewdness and cunning. To supply them Zeus needs the alliance of another character, Prometheus (also termed a Titan, though he actually belongs to the second generation; he is the son of the Titan Iapetus); Prometheus can bring Zeus the very thing the young god still lacks: cunning. That *metis*—a shrewd and wily mind—makes it possible to engineer events in advance so that they happen the way one wants them to.

Gaia, that great mother at once dark and luminous, mute and highly loquacious, informs Zeus that, to win, he must recruit certain beings who have the same parentage as the Titans but are not in their camp: She means the three Cyclopes and the three Hecatonchires. For those Titan gods are primordial deities who still retain the enormous brutality of natural forces; to vanquish and subdue the powers of disorder, she tells Zeus, it is necessary that he himself acquire the energy of disorder himself. Beings who are purely rational and orderly will never manage it; Zeus needs allies who embody the same capacity for violent brutality and passionate disorder as the Titans do.

So Zeus unbinds and releases the Cyclopes and the Hecatonchires from their underworld prison, and from then on they are inclined to come to his aid. But still the conflict is not over. To make loyal supporters of them, Zeus will have to do more than restore their freedom of movement after bringing them back from the dim dark jail where Cronus had hidden them away; he must also guarantee that if they fight alongside him, they will be entitled to nectar and ambrosia—that is, to the foods of immortality.

Once again, here is the food theme that has already been so prominent: Cronus devoured his children with fierce appetite, making food of them; he was so intent on filling his belly that when he was handed a stone dressed as an infant he gulped that down as well. The Hecatonchires and Cyclopes have the same parentage as the Titans; Zeus makes them into real Olympian deities by granting them the privilege of a food of immortality. For what characterizes the Olympian gods is that unlike animals, who eat all kinds of things, and unlike humans, who take their nourishment from bread and wine and ritually sacrificed meat, the gods need not feed to live—or rather, they ingest the foods of immortal life suited to their inner vitality, which, unlike men's, never runs down, never tires. After exertion men are hungry and thirsty; they must recharge their batteries. The gods are free from this constant concern. On the contrary, they have a kind of perpetual existence. Giving nectar and ambrosia to the Hecatonchires and the Cyclopes is confirmation that they really do number among the deities, in the full sense of the term. So: Shrewdness and cunning from the one bunch; and from the other, brute force and violence and the unleashing of disorder—using the Cyclopes and the Hundred-Armed Creatures, Zeus is able to turn those qualities back against the Titan gods who embody them. In the end, after ten "long years" of fluctuating combat, the scales tip toward Zeus and the other Olympians.

Who are the Cyclopes? How do they bring Zeus his victory? By providing him with an irresistible weapon—the thunderbolt. Gaia, who is still present, gives them the means to manufacture it, just as she mustered from her gut the steely white metal for the sickle that Cronus used to castrate his father Uranus. Here again she provides the material. The one-eyed Cylopes, like smiths—versions of Hephaestus before the fact—possess the thunderbolt, and they put it at Zeus's disposal to use at will. In Zeus's hand, it is an unimaginably powerful and intense compression of light and fire. That the Cyclopes should each have just a single eye is understandable: The eye itself is like fire. For the ancients—for the people who thought up these stories—a gaze is a person's essential light beaming from the eye. But the light that springs from Zeus's eye is actually lightning. Whenever he is in real danger, his eye blasts a bolt down on his adversaries. A Cyclops had his eye, and a Hecatonchire—one of those monsters of terrifying size and a hundredfold strength—had his arms (or hands: the Greek term *cheires* makes no distinction). The Hecatonchires with their hundred hands are the fist—the force. And now, with these two advantages—the Cyclopes' blasting eye and the power of the conquering arm—Zeus becomes truly invincible.

There is a culminating point in that battle. At the peak of combat between the divine powers, when Zeus shoots out his thunderbolt and the Hecatonchires attack the Titans, the world falls back into a chaotic state. The mountains crumble, chasms gape open, and from the depths of Tartarus, Night's kingdom, a mist suddenly rises from the depths. The sky collapses onto the earth, things return to the state of Chaos, to the primitive condition of primeval disorder, before things had any form. Zeus's victory is not merely a way of conquering his adversary and father, Cronus; it is also a way of re-creating the world, remaking an orderly world out of Chaos, out of a Void where nothing is visible, where all is disorder.

It is very clear that one of Zeus's strengths, whether through the hands of the Hundred-Armed Giants or through the Cyclopes' single eyes, is his ability to subdue the adversary, to impose his yoke upon him. Zeus's sovereignty is that of a king who possesses the magic of bondage: When an adversary rises up before him, Zeus snaps the shining whip of his gaze, and his lightning lassoes the target. Eye power, arm power—and the enemy falls, overcome. At the instant of that dreadful explosion of Zeus's power, which involves a temporary return to Chaos, the Titans are flung to the ground. Zeus fells them beneath the lashing of his thunderbolts and the Hecatonchires' terrible grip. They fall to earth, and the Hundred-Armed Creatures bury them beneath a mountain of enormous rocks; the Titans cannot move. These deities' power had always been expressed by their mobility, their constant presence; now they are reduced to nothing, immobilized and imprisoned under a mass they cannot escape. Their power no longer functions. The Hecatonchires seize them and carry them down to the underworld. The Titans cannot be killed—they are immortal—but they are relegated to the underworld, Chaos, to the mists of Tartarus, where nothing is distinct, where there is no direction; a gaping void open to the depths of the earth. To bar them from making their way back to the surface, Zeus orders Poseidon to build a rampart across the pass deep in the earth that provides a narrow pathway to the murky underground world of Tartarus. Through that pass, as through the neck of a jar, thread all the roots that the earth sets down in the shadows to hold it steady. There Poseidon builds a triple wall of bronze, and posts the Hundred-Armed Creatures as Zeus's stalwart guards. With the gateway blocked, every last precaution has been taken to ensure that that generation of Titans can never climb into the light again.

THE SOVEREIGNTY OF ZEUS

Thus ends the first act. Zeus is now victorious. He has won the support of the Cyclopes and of the Hundred-Armed Creatures, and even the allegiance of certain Titans—in particular, the goddess Styx, who represents all the menacing powers of the underworld, the infernal world, and the watery world too. She flows through the depths of the earth, she flows through Tartarus; then at a certain point she rises up to the surface. The waters of the Styx are so powerful that any mortal who tries to drink from it is instantly struck dead. In the course of the battle, Styx decided to quit the Titans' camp, where she belongs by origin, and join Zeus. Taking her place beside him, she brings along her two offspring, Kratus and Bie. Kratus represents the power to vanquish, the power to subjugate and rule the adversary; Bie embodies the brute violence that is the opposite of cunning. After his victory over the

Titans, Zeus keeps the two with him constantly: Kratus, the power of universal domination, and Bie, the capacity for unleashing overwhelming violence. When- and wherever Zeus goes, Kratus and Bie always flank him right and left.

Seeing this, the Olympian gods—his brothers and sisters—decide that the scepter shall go to Zeus. The Titans have paid the price of their infamy, and now Zeus assumes sovereignty. He parcels out privileges and honors among the gods. He establishes a divine universe that is hierarchical, ordered, organized, and that will therefore be stable. The world stage is constructed, the scenery is set. At its summit reigns Zeus, the organizer of the world brought out of Chaos.

Other questions arise. Uranus and Cronus are alike in many respects. Both are notable for the fact that they were unwilling to have their offspring replace them: Both prevented their progeny from emerging into the light. Each of these early gods stood as one celestial stratum refusing to let the next succeed it in the parade of generations. But apart from these similarities, in character Uranus is nothing like Cronus, from the standpoint of fable or story. Uranus, who was procreated by Gaia, later couples with her endlessly; his sole purpose is sexual union with her who bore him, in a ceaseless coitus. Uranus is utterly without guile; he is defenseless. He never for a moment considers that Gaia might want revenge on him.

Cronus also imprisons his offspring—not in their mother's belly as Uranus did, but in his own. Uranus was following his primitive Eros instinct, and it paralyzed him, keeping him fixated on Gaia. For Cronus, though, every move is governed by his determination to hold on to power, to remain the sovereign ruler. Cronus is the first politician. Not only is he the first king of the gods, the first king in the universe; he is also the first one to think in a crafty, political way for fear of losing his scepter.

Under Zeus a different sort of universe takes shape. His peers have chosen to make him king, and with punctilious fairness he metes out honors to them according to their deserts. He even continues the prerogatives of certain Titans who held them before he came to power, and who did not baldly join one side or the other during the gods' conflict. Ocean, for instance—Oceanus, the stream that circles the world—never declared for either the Titans or the Olympians. So, although he remained neutral, he will continue to oversee the outer boundaries of the world as he grips it in his liquid ring.

Zeus continues, and even increases, the many prerogatives of Hecate, a female divinity who also kept clear of the hostilities. True, Hecate does have a special position in the distribution of powers Zeus commands. She is not specifically either celestial or terrestrial; in the rigidly ordered world of male gods, she represents a notion of play, of pleasure, of chance. She may favor a person or destroy him, for no clear reason. Hecate grants fortune or misfortune as she pleases. In the waters she determines whether or not the fishes fare well, in the sky the birds, and on earth the cattle. She embodies an element of the gratuitous in the divine world; she brings a touch of the random. Both Zeus and Gaia see out over time, they know in advance how things are going to happen; Hecate greases the gears a little, she lets the world function more freely, with some margin of the unforeseen. Her prerogatives are enormous.

Now it would seem that everything is settled, but of course that is not so. The new generation of deities is in place. At its head stands Zeus, king of the gods, who has not merely succeeded Cronus but is his opposite. Cronus was nonjustice; he utterly disregarded his allies, whereas Zeus bases his reign on a kind of fairness, with some concern for equality in the way he treats the other divinities. He corrects for those elements in Cronus's rule that were biased, personal, harmful. Zeus establishes a more moderate, better-balanced form of sovereignty.

Time passes. Zeus has children, and, of course, those children quickly grow up and become very strong and powerful. Now, something in the way the world works presents a threat to the divine universe. To become adult, creatures must grow up, and time takes its toll on all things: Zeus himself was once a tiny babe in swaddling clothes, wailing in his grotto hiding place, protected by bodyguards. Now here he is in his prime—but won't he too suffer a decline? Doesn't the time come, for gods as it does for men, when the old king senses that he is no longer quite what he was; when beside him he sees his young son, whom he used to protect, becoming stronger than he and succeeding where he now falters? Will that not happen to Zeus himself? Just as Cronus dethroned his father, Uranus, and then Zeus did his father, Cronus, won't Zeus in his turn be dethroned by a son? Well, yes, that could—even must—occur; it does seem preordained in the order of time. Gaia knows this; so does Rhea. And Zeus, alerted, must gird himself against that eventuality. The system he has established must be such that it cannot be unsettled by a battle of succession for the throne. He has become king of the gods, master of the world—Zeus cannot be an ordinary sovereign. He must embody the very principle of sovereignty, the power of permanent and definitive rule. One key to such stability, to an unshakable reign replacing a string of transitory reigns, lies in marriage for the sovereign god.

THE RUSES OF POWER

Zeus's first wife bears the name Metis, which—we have seen—means that form of wisdom that won him his throne: Metis is shrewdness or cunning, the ability to foresee everything, never to be caught short or taken aback, never to leave one's flank exposed to unexpected attack. So Zeus marries Metis, and soon she is pregnant with Athena. But Zeus is afraid she might bear a son who will dethrone him in turn as he did his father Cronus. How to avoid this? Here is the swallowing theme again. Cronus swallowed his children, and yet he did not get to the root of the danger, since through a *metis*—a hoax—he was made to drink an emetic that forced him to vomit them all up again. Zeus has a far more radical solution: It is not enough to have Metis beside him as spouse; he has to *become* Metis himself. He doesn't need a partner, a companion; what he needs is to be the *metis* in person. How can he do it?

Metis has the power to transform herself; like various marine deities, she can take any shape. She can turn herself into a wild animal, an ant, a rock, whatever. A duel of wits develops between the spouses, Metis and Zeus. Who will win?

We have good reason to expect Zeus to use a maneuver we have seen in other situations. What is that? Naturally, when it comes to outdoing a very talented and powerful sorcerer or magician, a direct confrontation is doomed to fail. However, a craftier approach may just have a chance of working. Zeus questions Metis: "Are you really able to take any shape at all? Could you for instance turn into a fire-spitting lion?" And on the instant Metis becomes a fire-spitting lioness. A terrifying sight.

Then Zeus asks, "Could you even turn yourself into a—say—a drop of water?"

"Of course I can."

"Show me." No sooner does she become a drop of water than he gulps it down. And now Metis is trapped inside Zeus's belly. Cunning has worked again. This king is not content merely to swallow his prospective successors; instead, from now on, over the course of time, over the temporal flux, he is the incarnation of the cunning foresight that allows him to thwart the plan of anyone who might hope to surprise him, to catch him off guard.

His spouse, Metis, pregnant with Athena, is now inside his belly. So Athena will emerge not from her mother's loins but from her father's big head, which has become swollen like Metis's belly. Zeus is howling with pain. Prometheus and Hephaestus are called to the rescue. They come running with a battle-ax; they hit Zeus a great blow to the skull. With a huge cry Athena bursts from the god's head—a young virgin fully armed, with her helmet, her spear, her shield, and her bronze breastplate: Athena, the clever, inventive goddess. And meantime the cunning of the world is now all concentrated within Zeus's person. He is safe; no one can take him by surprise ever again. So the great problem of sovereignty is solved. The world of the gods has a leader whose authority can never again be open to question, because he is sovereignty itself. Nothing can threaten the cosmic order now. All is well once Zeus swallows Metis and thereby becomes the Metioeis—the god who is fully *metis*: resourcefulness personified.

UNIVERSAL MOTHER AND CHAOS

So now the war of the gods is over. The Titans are vanquished, the Olympians are victors. Actually nothing is resolved, because after Zeus's victory—when it seems that the world is finally at peace, that there reigns an order that is definitive and stable and just—

Gaia gives birth to a new creature called Typhoeus, or Typhon. She conceived him in a love match—tradition says "Golden Aphrodite" had urged it—with a male figure named Tartarus, the chasm deep within her—a kind of successor, an echo, of the primordial Chaos. Underground, mist-ridden, murky as night, Tartarus comes of a lineage completely different from the celestial powers that are the Olympian gods, or even the Titans.

The Titans had barely been banished from the heavens and sent down to the depths of the land of Tartarus to be closed away there forever, when Gaia decided—for the sake of bearing a new and final child—to couple with that same Tartarus whose realm lies at the farthest extreme from the sky. Gaia herself is the floor of the world, situated halfway between the brilliant heavens and murky Tartarus: If a bronze anvil were dropped from the height of the sky, it would take nine days and nine nights to reach the earth on the tenth day; that anvil falling from the earth downward would take the same time again to reach the land of Tartarus. In creating Uranus, and then in sexual congress with him, Gaia begat the whole line of the celestial gods. The universal mother, she conceives all and foresees all. She possesses oracular gifts and a form of foreknowledge that allows her, for instance in time of war, to show her favorites the secret, hidden, wicked means to victory. But Gaia is just as much the dark earth, the fogbound earth. There is still something of chaos in her, something primitive. She is not quite at home among those gods camped out in the shining empyrean, up where never the faintest cloud appears. She feels she does not get the respect she deserves from those characters who— from Othrys's peak to Olympus's—keep clashing ruthlessly over ruling the world.

In the beginning, we recall, there was Chaos. Then Gaia, the universal mother; she is actually the opposite of Chaos, but at the same time she bears some resemblance to Chaos; not only because

deep down—what with Tartarus and Erebus—she harbors some-
thing chaotic, but also because she comes into being right after
Chaos. Except for her, nothing else exists in the cosmos but
Chaos.

Typhon, the creature she brings forth out of this love match
with Tartarus, and who later destabilizes not just Zeus but the
whole godly system of Olympus, is a chthonic or "terrestrial"
being: *Chthon* is the term for the earth in its brooding, dark
aspect, rather than the earth as mother, as the sturdy ground for
all the beings who walk upon and draw their support from it. This
monstrous figure that Gaia produces is a singular creature:
Gigantic, primordial, he has both human and nonhuman qualities.
Fearfully strong, he contains the power of Chaos, of the primordial, of disorder. He has limbs as powerful as those of the
Hundred-Armed Creatures: arms slung from his shoulders with an
awesome vigor, flexibility, power. His feet grip the ground firmly;
they are tireless and forever active. He is a creature of action, of
motion. He is not like one of those monsters in some myths from
the Middle East, a heavy inert mass that grows large only once in
a while and functions simply as a resistant force that threatens to
block all the space between earth and sky. No, Typhon is always
moving and striking and flailing his legs and feet. He has a hundred serpent-heads—but a hundred serpent-heads each with a
black tongue stretching from its mouth. And each of those hundred heads has a pair of eyes that shoot forth a scorching flame, a
brilliance that both lights up those serpent-heads and at the same
time consumes whatever they look upon.

And what does he have to say, this hideous monster? He uses
many voices; sometimes he speaks the language of the gods, sometimes of humans. Other times he utters the cries of every wild
beast imaginable: He roars like a lion, he bellows like a bull. And
his voice, his way of speaking, are as multiform and varied and

motley as his whole look is grotesque. His figure signals not so much one particular quality as a jumble of all kinds of things, a conjunction of the most contrasting qualities and incompatible traits in one individual. If that monstrosity—so chaotic in appearance, in sound, in gaze and activity and power—had been victorious, then Zeus's system would have been destroyed.

After the war between the gods, and Zeus's accession to the throne, the birth of Typhoeus/Typhon constitutes a serious danger to the Olympian system. His victory would mean the regression of the world to the primordial, chaotic condition. What would have happened? The long struggle among the gods would be nullified. The world would return to a kind of chaos. Not by falling back into the primordial chaos of the beginnings—since out of that one an organized world had already emerged—but by collapsing into a general shambles.

TYPHON: THE CRISIS OVER SUPREME POWER

Typhon launches an attack on Zeus. The battle is terrifying. As in the struggle between the Titans and the Olympians, Zeus wins by making a kind of earthquake, an upheaval of the elements. The waters flood the land, the mountains crumble when Zeus thunders in his efforts to smash, to conquer the monster with his blast. In the very heart of Hades, the chasm of the dead and of night, everything churns together, all is yawning void. Typhon's struggle with Zeus is the struggle of the monster with hundreds of blazing eyes against the lightning flare of the divine gaze. Of course Zeus's blasting eye, with the light it projects, will prevail over the flames thrown by the monster's hundred serpent-heads. Eyes against eye. Zeus wins.

There is an anecdote that tells how Zeus once made the mistake of dropping his guard and drowsing off in his palace, despite that eye of his, said to be forever vigilant. Typhon sneaks up, sees where Zeus has laid down his thunderbolt, and is about to seize it—but just as he reaches for the weapon of victory, Zeus opens his eyes and blasts his enemy away. Two powers in opposition, Chaos and Olympus: Which will defeat the other by his vigilance and glare? In the end Typhon is vanquished yet again. The sinews of his arms and legs, which in him embody the life force as fighting spirit—these are destroyed by the thunderbolt. He is paralyzed, buried under boulders, and thrust back down into mist-shrouded Tartarus, whence he came.

Other, rather curious tales express Typhon/Typhoeus's monstrous nature in another way. These stories come from later periods, from the second century A.D. The differences between this character and Hesiod's Typhoeus, from the seventh century B.C., derive largely from Eastern influences.

In one, for instance: Weary of the Olympian gods, Gaia couples with Tartarus and conceives the monster Typhon. This beast is described as an enormous colossus, feet planted heavily into the ground, and endowed with a boundless body: His brow hits the sky, and when he spreads his arms, one hand touches the far East, the other the far West. In his own being he brings together and mixes high and low, sky and earth, right and left, Orient and Occident. This chaotic mass mounts an assault on Olympus. When the Olympians spot him, they are seized with irresistible terror; they turn into birds and fly away. Zeus is left to face up alone to this immense brute, tall as the world and broad as the universe. His thunderbolt strikes Typhoeus/Typhon and forces the monster back. Then Zeus takes up the *harpē*—the sickle—and tries to finish him off, but he is fighting hand to hand, and this time it is Typhoeus who prevails, because with his massiveness he manages to surround Zeus and stop him dead. Typhoeus then cuts out the sinews from the king's arms and legs; he hoists Zeus's body onto his back and carries it off to deposit it in a cavern in Cilicia in Asia Minor. While he's at it, the monster also hides away Zeus's sinews and his thunderbolt.

Now, it might seem that all is lost, and that this time the victory goes to the universe of total disorder. Indeed, the brute quits there, perfectly content, and confident that he has put poor Zeus away in that cavern, incapable of movement, empty of energy, stripped of his thunderbolt, the sinews cut out of his arms and legs.

But once again cunning, wiliness, deceit, trickery, intelligence carry the day for Zeus and his Olympians. Two characters—Hermes and Aegipan—use such means: Unnoticed by a sleeping Typhon, they manage to retrieve Zeus's severed sinews. Zeus slips them into place again as if he were putting on suspenders, and he snatches back his thunderbolt. When Typhon wakes and discovers that Zeus is gone from the cavern, the battle resumes stronger than ever, but it ends in utter defeat for the monster.

Other, similar versions tell how Zeus is temporarily conquered, taken prisoner, left without his strength or his thunderbolt. But his cunning companion Cadmus thwarts the monster's tactics. Typhon, believing that the matter is settled, proclaims himself king of the universe and declares his intent to return the primordial gods to power. He means to free the Titans and obliterate Zeus's reign. A bastard king, a lame king—Typhon is the king of disorder dethroning Zeus, the king of justice. Then Cadmus starts playing his flute. Typhon admires the music; he listens, then gently drowses off and falls into a deep sleep. He recalls tales of how Zeus would carry off certain mortals and have them entertain him with their music and poetry. Typhon wants to do the same, and he invites Cadmus to become his bard—to sing not of Olympus but of Typhon's own chaos. Cadmus accepts, but on the condition that he be provided a better instrument, one that would let him sing as he plays. "What do you require?" asks Typhon. "A lyre, and I'd need strings for it." "I've got just the thing—some terrific strings," Typhon declares, and runs to fetch Zeus's sinews. Cadmus plays again, absolutely wonderfully. Typhon falls asleep, and Zeus seizes the chance to pull his sinews off the lyre; he fits them back into his body, snatches up the thunderbolt, and prepares again for combat. When Typhon—the countergod, the counterfeit monarch of the universe—awakes, Zeus is again in full possession of his capacities and ready to attack him. And conquer him.

There is still another story in which cunning plays out the same way, but in this one Typhon is seen not as a multiform beast or a colossus, but as an aquatic animal, a terrifying whale, who fills up the entire space of the ocean. Typhon lives in an underwater cave, where he cannot be fought because Zeus's thunderbolt cannot reach the bottom of the sea. Once again, a trick upends the situation. Typhon is known to be an animal with a very big appetite, so Hermes, the patron god of fishermen (he taught his son Pan the skill), cooks up a feast of fishes to lure the sea monster out. Typhon does indeed emerge from his lair, and he stuffs his belly so full that when he tries to return to his den, he cannot get back through the door. Slumped on the beach, he makes an ideal target for Zeus, who now easily strikes him down.

These stories, perhaps a little weird, all involve the same lesson: Just when sovereignty seems definitively established, a crisis occurs over the supreme power. Some figure representing the very thing the new system was founded to correct—chaos, confusion, disorder—arises and threatens the master of the world. Zeus seems to be helpless. To take back his throne, he must call on some lesser figures. Unimpressive, hardly intimidating, these characters do not frighten the forces of disorder, who don't give them a second thought. But with their cunning, these minor gods or simple mortals help Zeus regain the upper hand and hold on to the supreme power.

Has Zeus finally achieved hegemony for good? Not yet. In fact, the business of establishing Zeus's supremacy involves still another episode, in the form of a battle with the characters called the Giants.

VICTORY OVER THE GIANTS

These are beings neither fully human nor fully divine; they have some intermediate status. The Giants are young warriors; in the universe, they symbolize the soldier function, the military system as different from Zeus's royal system. In their strength and violence they resemble the Hundred-Armed Creatures, who also have elements of that same warrior capacity. As we have seen, the Hundred-Armed Creatures have joined sides with Zeus; they submit to him and accept his authority. But the Giants, who represent armed might, pure violence, bodily vigor, physical youth—the Giants begin to wonder why they themselves shouldn't be the ones to hold the supreme power. This is the main thrust of the Giants' war.

The war is a highly perilous one, for they too were born of Earth, of Gaia. In many accounts, the Giants spring directly from Earth as full-grown adult fighters. They are never infants or little boys, no more than they are ever old men; right out of Earth, they already have the look of seasoned young soldiers. They come into the world fully armed, with the helmet and the hoplite trappings:

armor, javelin in one hand, sword in the other. No sooner are they born than they are battling one another; then they join forces and go to war against the gods. In that struggle, often described and pictured, the Olympians are shown joining against the Giants: Athena, Apollo, Dionysus, Hera, Artemis, Zeus—each fighting with his particular weapon. But Gaia tells Zeus that in the end the gods are not going to conquer their adversaries. And in fact, although the Olympians do inflict significant damage on their opponents, they do not manage to annihilate them. And despite their wounds and losses, the Giants keep up the attack.

The Giants' strength is the strength of a constantly replenished age cohort: young men just starting a military life. To beat them the gods of Olympus need an ally who is not divine. Once again Zeus is forced to turn to an ordinary mortal to vanquish the Giants. He probably has need of a mortal precisely because those young Giants, who were never children and who will never be old men, seem like humans. Yet they fight the gods, and the gods cannot wipe them out. They are midway between mortal and immortal. Their status is as unsettled as that of a young man in the flower of youth: not yet full-grown but no longer a child. Such are the Giants.

THE EPHEMERAL FRUITS

To bring off their campaign, the Olympians enlist the support of Heracles. He is not yet a god, he has not acceded to Olympus; he is merely the son of the union between Zeus and a mortal, Alcmene. He is himself a mortal. It is Heracles who will wreak havoc upon the race, the tribe, the *phylē* of the Giants. But despite these ravages, the devastation is not over. Once again Gaia plays an ambiguous role; she bore these creatures fully armed, and she does not want to see them destroyed. She thus goes off to find a certain night-sprouting herb said to provide immortality. She means to pluck it at dawn and give it to the Giants to make them immortal. For she wants the Olympians to acknowledge these rebellious youngsters, come to terms with them, and drop any plans for their destruction. But Zeus gets wind of Gaia's project and manages to foil it: Just before daybreak, before the light touches the ground and the plant is too easily visible, he harvests it. Never again will a leaf of that immortality plant be found any-where on earth. So the Giants will not be able to eat of it . . . and inevitably they will die.

This detail recalls another element, which is sometimes attrib-uted to the Giants' story and sometimes to Typhon's. The story goes that Typhon was searching for a *pharmakon*, a potion that is both medication and poison. This sort of potion, which can kill or cure, is in the hands of the Moirai—the Fates, female deities who preside over the assignment of destinies. They give Typhon a drug and tell him that it confers immortality; they promise him bound-less power and energy, and victory over Zeus. Typhon swallows the drink but, far from a "drug for immortality," what the god-desses have given him is an "ephemeral fruit"—that is, a plant meant for mortals to eat. It is the food of humans, creatures who live only from day to day, and whose powers wear out. The "ephemeral fruits" are the mark of mortality. Rather than nectar and ambrosia, rather than the sacrificial smoke that men send up to the gods, this "ephemeral" food makes Typhon fragile, vulner-able, like a human. Similarly the Giants experience fatigue and vulnerability; they do not have the constant, perpetually lively vitality the gods do.

In the background of all these stories is the notion of a heav-enly system without particular privileges for one deity or another.

Nectar and ambrosia are the alimentary markers of the immortals. Zeus grants the food of immortality to the Cyclopes and to the Hundred-Armed Creatures, making them full-fledged gods to stand beside him as allies. But to anyone seeking to wrest away his supreme power, Zeus offers only an "ephemeral" food—the food eaten by beings who are mortal and vulnerable. When, the course of battle, victory looks dubious, to swing it toward his Olympians Zeus readily has his adversaries eat food that will make them weak like men.

AT THE OLYMPIC TRIBUNAL

With Zeus's victory over the Giants, his reign finally appears to be firmly established; the gods who fought beside him will hold forever the prerogatives they were awarded. They have the heavens, where there is only light, pure light. At the bottom of the world are night and shadows, Tartarus or Hades: It is the abode of conquered gods, of monsters brought to heel, of the Giants reduced to immobility, tied up or put to sleep like Cronus. They are largely out of the running, out of the cosmos. Those gods aside, the world between contains beasts and men—creatures that experience both night and day, good and evil, life and death. Their life is bound up with death, like the foods they consume.

Observing the unfolding of this story, a certain idea emerges: For a differentiated world to exist, with its hierarchies and its organization, there had to be an initial act of rebellion: the one that Cronus carried out when he castrated Uranus. At the time Uranus hurled a curse on his children, a malediction that charged them with a crime that must be avenged, a *tisis*. And thus the course of time is a rocky one, with room in it for evil and vengeance, for the Erinyes (Furies) who enforce the expiation of crimes, for the Keres. It was the drops of blood fallen from Uranus's castrated organ that produced the forces of violence the wide world over. But things are more complicated, more ambiguous. Between the dark forces besieging the universe because of the mutilation of Uranus, that first foundational act toward creating an organized cosmos—between those forces and the forces of peace, there is some link. On one side the Erinyes, the Giants, and the nymphs of war, and on the other Aphrodite.

Chaos engendered Night, and Night gave birth to all the forces of evil. Those evil forces are death, the Parcae, the Keres— murder, slaughter, carnage—and all the misfortunes—Sorrow, Hunger, Fatigue, Strife, and Age. Among the miseries that burden the universe are Apate—deceit, and Philotes—sexual congress. Night bred both of those along with murder and slaughter. All those various dark female forces rush into the universe and turn the world from a harmonious place into a realm of terrors, of crimes, of vengeance, of falseness. But then if we consider Aphrodite's own descendants, there we also find evil forces alongside the benevolent. There are Eros and Himeros, desire and tenderness—all fine so far—but also the lies and deceits, *exapatai*, the seductive snares hidden in girls' prattle, and here again, erotic attachment—Philotes.

In Aphrodite's realm—the forces of union, accord, and gentleness—and in the progeny of a dark power begetting every possible misfortune, there are intersections and blendings and duplications: The children of Night include flirtatious talk and sexual congress, just as Aphrodite's own following includes a girl's fetching smiles alongside lies in lovemaking. A man who is duped and hoodwinked can run into trouble there. So things are not all white in the one camp and black in the other. This universe is continually generated from a mix of opposites.

By mobilizing the rage of the avenging powers, Night helps to bring clarity back to a system clouded by misdeeds. For her part, Aphrodite the luminous, Aphrodite the golden, has a counterpart black Aphrodite—*Melainis*—an Aphrodite of the night, murky, hatching her tricks in the darkness.

In the course of bringing order to the universe, Zeus takes particular care to exclude Night, darkness, conflict from the divine world. He creates a regime wherein, if the gods should quarrel, their dispute cannot erupt into wider conflict. He has banished war from the territory of the gods and sent it down to men. All the evil forces that Zeus expelled from the Olympian world become the ordinary fabric of human existence. He asked Poseidon to construct a triple bronze wall to close off the portal to Tartarus, to keep Night and the evil powers from ever again climbing up to the sky. They do exist in the world, of course; but Zeus has set up safeguards against them.

If a quarrel should arise among the gods, one that might grow dangerous, they are all brought together for an enormous banquet. Also invited is Styx, who arrives with a golden ewer filled with the water of the river of Hades. The two deities in conflict take hold of that ewer, pour some water onto the ground, make a libation; they drink of it as well, and each of them swears under oath that he or she is not responsible for the quarrel—that he is in the right. Naturally one of the two must be lying. No sooner does the liar god swallow the sacred water than he falls into a coma, a kind of deep lethargy. He goes into a state analogous to that of a conquered god: Like Typhon or the Titans, he has no breath or heat or vitality. He is not dead, for gods do not die, but he has lost everything connected to his nature as a god: He can no longer move or act, no longer exercise power, is out of commission. In a sense he is out of the cosmos, caught in a lethargy that sets him apart from divine existence. He remains in that state for a very long time, for a "long year." When he wakes from his coma, he is still not entitled to share in the banquet, or to drink nectar and ambrosia. That deity is neither mortal nor out-and-out immortal; he is in a situation like the Titans, the Giants, or Typhon: He is shut out.

In other words, in this multiple, diverse world of the gods, Zeus is alert to the dangers of a conflict. Keeping an eye out for trouble, he has set up not only a political system but also a quasi-juridical one, so that if a dispute should arise, it does not threaten to shake the very pillars of the world. The guilty deities will be expelled from Olympus until they have paid their penalty. Afterward, they wake from their lethargy, but they still have no right to the nectar or ambrosia; for that they must wait out another period ten times as long as the sentence. That is the rule among the gods, but not among men.

IRREPARABLE HARM

So Typhon is vanquished, undone by everything Zeus buried him under. Perhaps his corpse was dispatched to where the Titans were imprisoned before him—down in Tartarus, which would be only natural since Typhon is Tartarus's son. Or possibly he remains pinned under those enormous mountainous masses thrown onto him—under Mount Etna in particular: Typhon is entangled in Etna's roots, bound beneath the volcano that from time to time spouts smoke or boiling lava or flames. Are these the remains of Zeus's thunderbolt still flaring up? Or a fit of anomie from Typhon? If that really is he, acting up in these shudders of Etna, in that lava, out of those depths from which boiling matter bursts toward the surface, it would prove that what Typhon represents—

as a disordering power—has not totally vanished with his defeat, or even with his paralysis or death.

One version of this tale worth emphasizing has it that from Typhon's corpse come gales and squalls—which are expressions at the earth's surface, and especially the ocean's, of what Typhon would have meant for the universe if he had been victorious. If Typhon had won out over Zeus, an irreparable harm—an absolute evil—would have taken over the universe. Now that he is conquered, put out of commission, something of him persists nonetheless—not among the gods anymore, but among the poor human race. Out of Typhon, suddenly, without warning, come terrible winds that never blow in just one direction as other winds do. The Notos, the Boreus, or the Zephyr are steady winds, linked to the morning star or the evening star; in that sense, they are children of the gods. Those winds show sailors the navigation routes, they trace out great aerial roadways across the surface of land or sea. On the water, which is an infinite space like a liquid Chaos, those steady winds mark out reliable directions that help sailors find safe haven. Not only do these winds always blow in the same direction, but they are seasonal as well: The Boreus blows at one particular time, the Zephyr at another, so that when sailors must set forth they know which season is right for a voyage to this or that destination.

But the squalls, the fog-laden gales are something else entirely. When they hit the sea, nothing is visible. It is suddenly blackest night, which throws everything off course. Directions gone, fixed landmarks gone . . . these are whirlwinds that confuse everything. No more west or east, no up or down. Caught amid that chaotic sea world, ships lose their way and founder. Such winds come straight out of Typhon; they are the mark Typhon continues to stamp onto the universe, primarily on the seaways but on terra firma too. In fact, these utterly incomprehensible and unpredictable squalls do not blow only on the water. Some devastate whole harvests, throw down trees, obliterate all human labor. Farmlands and harvests, patiently prepared and stored, are reduced to nothing: Typhon is truly an irreparable harm.

So Zeus's victory does not put a complete end to Typhon's activity as chaotic energy in the cosmos. The Olympians threw him out of their sacred realm, but they sent him to live with men, where he brings discord, war, and death. The gods may have expelled from their own domain every element belonging to the world of the primitive, of disorder, but they have not annihilated it; they have only put it far away from themselves. Now Typhon is raging among men, with a brute violence that leaves them utterly defenseless. He is an irreparable evil against which, to use a phrase of the Greeks, there is no recourse.

THE GOLDEN AGE: MEN AND GODS

Zeus sits on the throne of the universe. The world is now in order. The gods have fought, and some of them have triumphed. Everything bad in the ethereal sky has been run out—either locked away below in Tartarus or sent to earth to the mortals. And humans—what is happening to them, what are they now?

The story begins not exactly at the start of the world, but at the moment when Zeus is already king—that is, in the period when the gods' world has been stabilized. The gods do not live only on Olympus; they share certain bits of the earth with humans. In particular there is a place in Greece near Corinth—a plain at Mecone—where gods and men live together. They share the same meals, they sit at the same tables, they feast together. Which means that, among the intermingled gods and men, every day is a holiday, a happy day. They eat, they drink, they make merry, they listen to the Muses sing the glory of Zeus and the adventures of the gods. In short, all goes well.

The Mecone plain is a land of wealth and abundance. Crops grow spontaneously there. As in the proverb, all a person needs is a plot of land in that valley for riches to pour in, for it never suffers the vicissitudes of bad weather or the seasons. A golden age, when gods and men were not yet separate; a golden age sometimes also later called "the time of Cronus"—that time before the start of the struggle between Cronus with his Titan allies, and Zeus with his Olympians—when the divine world is not yet given over to brutal violence. It is peace, a time before time. And men have their place in it. How do they live? Not only sitting down at the same table with the gods, but also without experience of any of the ills that nowadays beset the race of mortals, of ephemeral beings, of creatures who live from day to day never knowing what tomorrow will bring, nor feeling real continuity with what happened yesterday; who simply go on changing, being born, growing up, growing strong, growing frail, and dying.

Back then, men stayed young, their arms and legs forever the way they were from the start. For them, no birth as such: Perhaps they sprang from Earth. Perhaps Gaia, Earth Mother, brought them forth just as she had brought forth the gods. Perhaps—without asking where they came from—they were simply *there*, mingling with the gods and like the gods. So, back then, men were young forever and did not know birth or death. They were not affected by time, time that wears out a man's energies and makes him old. After hundreds or maybe myriads of years, still as they were in the flower of their youth, they would fall asleep, disappear as they had appeared. They were no more, but it was not really death. There was no toil back then either, or illness, or suffering. Men did not have to work the earth: At Mecone every foodstuff, every resource, was ready to hand. Life resembled what some legends say about the Ethiops: A sunny table awaits them every morning, and on it they find food and drink all set out for them. Not only are the foodstuffs and the meats there, always ready; not only do the crops spring up without sowing; but even the very meals come already cooked. Spontaneously and easily, nature provides all the goods of domestic life at its most refined, most civilized. That is the way men lived in those long-ago times—in contentment.

Women have not been created yet. The feminine does exist—there are goddesses—but no mortal women. Humans are exclusively male: Just as they are unfamiliar with illness or age or death or labor, so they do not know sexual congress with women. When the making of children comes to require a man to lie with a woman who is both like him and different from him, then birth and death become the lot of humankind. Birth and death make two stages of a life; for there to be no death, there must be no birth either.

At Mecone gods and men live together; they are joined, but the time has come to separate. That occurs after the gods have arranged their great distribution of powers among themselves. Violence surrounded their first efforts to work out the question of honors and prerogatives to be allotted each of them. The arrangement between the Titans and the Olympians was the end result of a struggle where force and brutal domination prevailed. With that first distribution completed, the Olympians dispatched the Titans down into Tartarus, locked the doors of the dark underworld prison, and went to live together high in the sky. They had to settle the problems among themselves. Zeus was charged with carrying out the allotment of powers—this time not by imposing it with brute force but by winning a consent agreement among all the Olympians. Among gods apportionment is done at the end of either an open conflict or an agreement, if not among equals then at least among allies and kinsmen committed to a common cause, engaged in the same battle.

The Human World

PROMETHEUS THE WILY

How to assign the relative positions of gods and men? Settling matters by brute force is no longer thinkable here. Humans are too weak; a mere flick of the finger would reduce them to nothing. But neither can the immortals negotiate an agreement with the mortals, as if between equals. Some solution must be found that depends neither on excessive force nor on an understanding among peers. To bring about such an arrangement—necessarily makeshift and skewed—Zeus calls on a figure named Prometheus. He also suits the bizarre method to be used for deciding between gods and men, for settling competition between them.

And why is Prometheus the right choice for the job? Because, in the world of the gods, his own status is ambiguous, ill defined, paradoxical. He is considered a Titan; actually he is the son of Cronus's brother Iapetus, so it is his father who is a Titan; Prometheus is not really one himself. But neither is he an Olympian, for he does not come from that stock. He does have the nature of a Titan—as does his brother Atlas. Zeus eventually comes to punish both of them.

Prometheus has a rebellious spirit, clever and insubordinate, and always quick to find fault. Why does Zeus give him the task of working out this business? Because, as a not-quite-Titan, Prometheus had not joined with the Titans fighting against Zeus. He adopted a neutral position, took no part in the struggle. In fact, several traditions say that Prometheus actually counseled Zeus, and that without his advice—since he is a trickster, a wily fellow—Zeus would not have won. In that sense he is an ally to Zeus. An ally, but not a recruit or a comrade in arms: He is not in Zeus's camp; he is autonomous, his own man.

Zeus and Prometheus have much in common with regard to intelligence and mentality. Both are known for subtle, crafty minds—for that same quality Athena represented among the gods, and Odysseus embodied among men—wiliness. The wily trickster manages to pull his coals out of the fire when the situation seems utterly desperate; he finds a way when every door is blocked; and to achieve his ends he has no compunction about lying or setting snares for the opponent or using every trick in the book. Zeus is like that and so is Prometheus; they share that quality. Still, there is an enormous distance between them: Zeus is a king, a ruler who holds total power in his own hands. On that count Prometheus is absolutely not in rivalry with Zeus. The Titans were the rivals of the Olympians, and Cronus the rival of Zeus, since he wanted to hold on to his throne when Zeus determined to become ruler in his stead. But Prometheus never imagines himself king; not for a moment is he competing with Zeus on that score. The world Zeus created—that world of allocated powers, that hierarchical world ranked by levels, by differences in status and honor—Prometheus belongs to that world, but his standing in it is rather difficult to define. And all the more complex in that Zeus later condemns him and orders him chained, then eventually releases him and reconciles with him: His personal destiny swings back and forth between hostility and harmony. One might say that within that orderly universe, Prometheus is an expression of internal dissent. He is not seeking to supplant Zeus, but within the system Zeus has established, Prometheus is that small voice of contention inside the gods' world—something of a 1968-style rebellion on Olympus.

Prometheus's relationship with men is one of complicity, of a common nature. His condition is similar to that of humans, because they too are ambiguous creatures: They contain both some strain of the divine—they did live side by side with the gods, early on—and at the same time a strain of animality, of bestiality. So both in men and in Prometheus, there are contradictory elements.

A CHESS GAME

Here is the scene: Gods and men are gathered as usual. Zeus is present, there in the front loges, and he commands Prometheus to work out the allocation of goods and privileges between the gods and men. What will Prometheus do? He brings in a great bovine, a splendid ox, which he slaughters and then butchers into parts. He makes up two portions, not three. As Prometheus prepares them, the portions will express the difference in status between gods and men. That is, the way the animal is butchered will delineate the divide between men and gods.

How does Prometheus do it? The way it is routinely done in Greek sacrifice: The animal is slaughtered, the hide stripped off, and then begins the butchering. In particular: A first step is to strip bare the long bones of the fore and rear limbs, the *ostea leuka*; they are trimmed so as to leave no meat on them. This accomplished, Prometheus gathers all those white bones together. He ties them into one bunch and wraps it in a thin layer of tempting white fat. That is one portion. Then he goes on to prepare a second. In this one Prometheus puts all the *krea*—the fleshy parts, everything that can be eaten, and that edible meat is wrapped in the animal's hide. Then this bundle—the rough hide holding all the edible food from the beast—is in turn wrapped in the animal's *gaster*, or stomach—the slimy, ugly, repellent belly sac.

So the division is as follows: one portion appetizing white fat wrapped around only bare white bones and the other, a somewhat disgusting stomach sac filled with all the good edible parts inside it. Prometheus lays the two portions on the table in front of Zeus. The king's choice will determine the dividing line between men and gods. Zeus looks at the two portions and says, "Ah! Prometheus, you're so crafty, so sly—and you've made the shares very different." Prometheus looks at him with a little smile. Zeus, of course, is aware of the ruse, but he goes along with the rules of the game. He is invited to choose first, and he agrees. Looking very confident, he picks the more appealing portion—the packet wrapped in succulent white fat. Everyone is watching; he undoes the packet and discovers the meatless white bones. He explodes in a horrific rage against this fellow who set out to trick him.

Thus ends the first act of this story, which has at least three. By the close of this episode, it is already determined how men will enter into relation with the gods: through sacrifice, like the one

Prometheus carried out in killing the animal. On the altar outside the temple, aromatic herbs are set afire and they send up a fragrant smoke; then white bones are laid on the branches. The gods' share is the white bones, shiny with grease, that rise up to the skies in the form of smoke. Men, meanwhile, get the rest of the animal, which they will consume either grilled or boiled. On long iron or bronze skewers they thread chunks of meat, notably the liver and some other appealing parts, and set them to grill directly on the flame. Still other chunks are put into great cauldrons to boil. Roast some cuts, boil others: Henceforward men must eat the meat of sacrificed animals and send the gods their share—that is, the fragrant smoke.

What's startling about this story is that it seems to show that Prometheus managed to fool Zeus and slip men the better part of the sacrifice. Prometheus provides men with the edible portion — camouflaged as something inedible, repugnant—and gives the gods the inedible portion, disguised in that delectable, gleaming layer of fat. His conduct is deceitful, for the appearance is misleading: The good is wrapped in the ugly and the bad in the beautiful.

But did Prometheus actually give men the better part? Here again things are ambiguous. Certainly mankind does get the edible share of the sacrificed beast—but that's because men need to eat. Their condition is the opposite of the gods'; they cannot live without continually feeding themselves. Men are not self-sufficient; they must draw energy from resources in the surrounding world, and without them they perish. What defines humans is that they eat bread and sacrificial meats, and that they drink the wine of the vine. The gods have no need to eat. They know not bread, or wine, or the flesh of sacrificed animals. They live without nourishment, they take in only pseudofoods, nectar and ambrosia, the foods of immortality. The gods' vitality is thus entirely different in nature from mankind's. Man's is a subvitality, a subexistence, a subforce: an energy with moments of eclipse. It requires constant refueling. As soon as a human being puts forth some effort he feels tired, exhausted, used up, hungry. In other words, in the distribution Prometheus has worked out, the better share is indeed the one that hides meatless bones within the more appetizing package. Because actually, in the beast or the human, the white bones are the thing that is truly precious, that is nonmortal, that does not die; bones do not decay, they form the architecture of the body. The flesh disintegrates, decomposes, but the skeleton represents permanence; what is inedible in the animal is what is not mortal, what is immutable—what therefore comes closest to the divine. For the people who invented these stories, the bones are all the more important because they contain the marrow, that substance the Greeks saw as linked both to the brain and to the semen. The marrow represents an animal's continuing vital force down through the generations; it ensures fecundity and progeny. It is the sign that one is not an isolated individual but a bearer of offspring.

So in the end, what the gods get through Prometheus's hoax is the animal's life force, whereas what men receive—the meat—is only dead animal. Men must nourish themselves by a chunk of dead animal; and this division marks them for good as mortal in nature. Humans are henceforward the mortals, the ephemeral creatures, as opposed to the gods, who are nonmortals. Through this distribution of foodstuffs, humans bear the stamp of mortality, while the gods bear that of perpetuity. Which Zeus clearly understood.

If Prometheus had simply made up two portions, with the bones on one side and the meat on the other, Zeus might anyhow have chosen the bones—and thus the vital force—of the beast. But since everything was distorted by misleading appearances, since the meat was hidden inside the *gaster* and the bones disguised in glistening fat, Zeus saw that Prometheus had meant to fool him. So he decided to punish him. Naturally, in this battle of cunning between Zeus and the "Titan" Prometheus, each of them is looking to outwit the other, each is playing against the other like a chess match, with underhanded gambits to confound the opponent, to put him in check and mate. It is a contest that Zeus ultimately wins, but he is thrown off balance by the Titan's maneuvers.

A FATAL FIRE

In the second act Prometheus will have to pay for his skullduggery. Zeus decides to withhold both fire and grain from mankind. As in a chess game, each move is a response to another: Prometheus had hidden the meat in a repugnant covering and the bones in an appetizing one, and now Zeus takes his revenge. In the context of dividing things up between gods and men, Zeus decides to deprive men of what had previously been available to them. Till then men had had ready access to fire, because Zeus's fire—the fire of the thunderbolt—could be found at the top of certain trees, ash trees, and men could simply take it. The same fire moved back and forth between gods and men by means of these great trees, where Zeus would deposit it. Thus men had access to fire as they did to foods, to cereals that grew spontaneously and meats already cooked on arrival. Now Zeus is hiding fire away—a situation all the more troublesome because men do have the meat of sacrificed animals, and they would like the means to cook it. Mortals are not cannibals or wild animals who eat raw meat. They cannot eat meat unless it is cooked, either boiled or roasted.

To be left without fire is a catastrophe for men. Zeus is delighted. Prometheus thereupon works up a response. His manner offhand, he goes up to the sky and, like any traveler, strolls about with a staff in hand—in this case, a branch of giant fennel, fresh green on the outside. Fennel has a peculiar feature: Its structure is somewhat opposite to that of other trees. Most are dry outside, at the bark, and moist inside, where the sap circulates; but fennel is moist and green outside and utterly dry on the inside. Prometheus steals a seed from Zeus's fire (*sperma puros*) and slips it into the hollow core of his fennel stalk. The fire begins to burn through the whole center of the stalk. Prometheus goes back down to earth, still looking like a casual traveler walking along beneath his lacy-topped fennel-stalk umbrella. But inside the plant, the fire is seething—this fire drawn from a seed of the celestial fire Prometheus gives to men. With it they light their homes and cook their meat. Zeus, lounging about up in the sky, pleased with his move in concealing the fire, suddenly sees its flame glowing in all the houses down on earth. He flies into a fury. Note that Prometheus is using the same mechanism in this instance as he did in dividing up the sacrificial beast: Again he is playing on the contrast between inside and outside, the difference between external appearance and internal fact.

When he withheld fire from mankind, Zeus also concealed *bios*, life—that is to say, the nourishment that supports life: the cereals, wheat, barley. He has stopped providing fire, and he has stopped providing grains as well. Back in "the Cronus period," the Golden Age in the Mecone Plain world, man had had free use of the fire atop the ash trees, grain grew of its own accord, and there was no need to till the earth. Labor did not exist, there was no toil. Man was not obliged to take an active role in producing food for himself. He was not forced to effort or fatigue or exhaustion in acquiring the nourishment on which his very vitality depended. Now, by Zeus's decision, what had been spontaneous has become laborious, difficult. The grain is withheld.

Just as Prometheus had to conceal a seed of fire inside his stalk to bring it home to men, from now on men must hide the seeds of wheat and barley in the belly of the earth. There in the earth's basin they must plow a furrow and lay in the seed in order for the plant to sprout. In short, agriculture suddenly becomes necessary. Man now has to earn his bread by the sweat of his brow, perspiring over the furrows, sowing the seeds. But he will also have to think about saving seed from year to year—not eating everything he has grown. Containers will be needed in the farmer's house for storing some portion of the harvest, which cannot be totally consumed: A reserve stock is now indispensable, so that in springtime, at the difficult juncture between winter and the new crop, men are not left destitute.

There was the *sperma* of fire, and there is the *sperma* of wheat. Men are now obliged to live by labor. They do get a kind of fire back, but like the wheat, it is different from before. The fire Zeus hid away is celestial fire, the one he keeps perpetually in his hand, a fire that never falters, never fails: an immortal fire. The fire men have now at their disposal, the fire from that fire-seed, because it does come from a seed, is a fire that is "born"—so it is also a fire that dies; it must be kept burning, it must be tended. This fire has an appetite like mortal man's; unless it is constantly fed, it goes out. Men need it not just to warm themselves but in order to eat: Unlike animals, they do not eat their meat raw, they cook—and cooking follows a ritual whose rules require the use of fire.

For the Greeks wheat is a plant that is "cooked"—primarily by the sun's heat, but also by man's labor. Then it must be cooked again at the bakery, by putting it in the oven. So fire is truly the marker of human culture. This Promethean fire, stolen away by trickery, is in fact a "technological" fire—an intellectual process that distinguishes man from beasts and consecrates his nature as a civilized creature. And yet insofar as this human fire needs constant fresh fuel to live, unlike divine fire, it is also something like a wild beast that, once unleashed, cannot stop. It burns everything, not only the food we give it but houses and cities and forests as well; it is a kind of flaming beast, with a ravenous, unappeasable hunger. In its highly ambiguous nature, fire underlines what is specific to man: It constantly recalls both his divine origin and his animal nature; it partakes of both—like man himself.

PANDORA: THE INVENTION OF WOMAN

Now the story would seem to be complete. But no—the third act begins. Indeed, men do have civilization now; Prometheus has provided them the necessary technology. Before he intervened they were living like ants in caves—they would look without seeing, listen without hearing, they were nothing—and then, thanks to him, they became civilized beings, distinct from the beasts and distinct from the gods.

But the battle of wiles between Zeus and Prometheus is not over. Zeus withheld fire, Prometheus stole it from him; Zeus withheld grain, men must labor to earn their bread. But Zeus is not satisfied yet; to his mind his adversary is not totally defeated. Roaring with laughter, as he loves to do, Zeus has a new setback in store for Prometheus. Act Three.

Zeus calls together Hephaestus, Athena, Aphrodite, and some minor deities like the Hours (the Horai). He commands Hephaestus to moisten some clay with water and to model a sort of figure in the shape of a *parthenos*, a woman—more precisely a maiden—a woman ready for marriage but not yet married, and especially not having yet borne a child. So Hephaestus sets about molding a figure, a statue, with a lovely virgin's pleasing features. Next he calls on Hermes to bring the thing to life and endow it with the strength and the voice of a human being, along with other details that will appear later in the story. Zeus then asks Athena and Aphrodite to dress her, make her still more beautiful with the glory of finery appropriate to a female body—ornaments, jewels, bodices, headdresses. Athena garbs her in a superb costume—brilliant and gleaming like the white fat enfolding the bones back at the start of this story. The young virgin glows. On her head Hephaestus sets a diadem with a marriage veil flowing from it. The diadem is trimmed with an animal border showing all the beasts in the world—birds and fishes, tigers and lions—and the girl's brow beams with their vitality. She is splendid to behold— *thauma idesthai*, a marvel that leaves the witness transfixed, stupefied, and totally enamored.

And there stands Pandora, the first woman, before gods and men assembled. It is a figure that is fabricated but not drawn from a woman as such—since there are none yet. *She* is the first, the archetype of woman. The *feminine* did already exist, since there were goddesses; this feminine creature is shaped like a *parthenos*, in the image of immortal goddesses. The gods create a being out of earth and water, and into it put a man's strength, *sthenos*, and a human voice, *phōnē*. But Hermes also puts lying words in her mouth, gives her the mentality of a bitch and a thieving temperament. This mannequin—the first woman, the figure from whom will descend the whole "race of women"—presents a misleading exterior, like the two portions from the sacrificial beast, or the hollow fennel stalk. No one can gaze upon her without being enchanted, rooted to the spot. She possesses the beauty of the immortal goddesses; her appearance is divine. Hesiod says it well: One is . . . dazzled. Her beauty, enhanced by the jewels and the diadem, the gown and the veil, is ravishing. *Charis* beams from her—a boundless allure, a radiance that overwhelms and conquers anyone who sees her. Her *charis* is infinite, multiple—*polle charis*. Men and gods all fall under her spell. Inside, though, something else is hidden. Her voice enables her to become man's companion, his human match; they will converse together. However, this woman is given speech not for telling truth and expressing her feelings, but for telling falsehoods and camouflaging her emotions.

Night's descendants include all the evils: death, slaughters, and the Erinyes, of course; but also some things that could be translated as "lying or seductive words," "sexual congress or sexual feeling." Now, since her birth, Aphrodite's attributes have always included lying words and sexual appeal too. The darkest and brightest, the gladdest thing and the direst conflict commingle in these falsehoods, this sexual seduction. This is Pandora, then: radiant like Aphrodite and also, like a child of Night, made up of lies and coquetry. Zeus is creating this *parthenos* not for the gods but exclusively for mortals. Just as Zeus had rid himself of conflict and violence by handing them down to mortals, now he means to send man this female figure.

Prometheus sees he is beaten again. He understands instantly what's being dangled before the nose of the poor human race that he has been trying to help. As his name "Pro-metheus" indicates, he is foresighted, the one who understands a situation beforehand, who anticipates; whereas his brother, "Epi-metheus," is the one who understands only afterward—*epi*, too late—who is always taken in and let down, who never sees it coming. The rest of us poor miserable mortals—we are always both Prometheans and Epimetheans at once; we look ahead, we make plans—and very often events turn out differently from what we expected: They take us by surprise and leave us defenseless. In this case Prometheus sees what is going to occur and he warns his brother: "Listen, Epimetheus: If ever the gods send you a gift, absolutely do not accept it; send it right back where it came from." Epimetheus swears of course that he won't be fooled. But then the assembled gods send him the loveliest person in the world. Before him stands Pandora, the gods' gift to mankind. She knocks at his door, and Epimetheus—in wonderment, bedazzled—opens it to her and brings her into his home. The next day he is married, and Pandora is established as a wife among the humans. And thus begin all their miseries.

Now humankind is twofold, no longer made up of just the masculine gender. The race comprises two different sexes, both necessary to human propagation. From the moment the gods produce woman, men are no longer simply *there*, from one moment to the next; now they are born of women. To reproduce, mortals must couple—which fact sets off a new process in time.

Why is it that, according to the Greek stories, Pandora, the first woman, has a bitch's mentality and a thieving temperament? This is not unrelated to the two first parts of this tale. Men no longer have access to grain and fire as they did before, quite naturally and effortlessly and always. Toil is now part of existence; men lead lives that are nasty, brutish, and short. They must always exercise restraint. The peasant in his field works himself to death and scrapes out only a paltry harvest. Men never have enough of anything; they must be frugal, cautious about spending any more than necessary. Now, the stories show this Pandora, like her whole *genos*—the whole "race" of feminine women who descend from her—with a particular characteristic: She is always dissatisfied, demanding, self-indulgent. She is never content with what there is; she wants to be sated, surfeited. That is what the story means when it says that Hermes gave her the mentality of a bitch. Her bitchery is of two sorts. First, alimentary: Pandora has a voracious appetite, she never stops eating, she must always be sitting at the table. Perhaps she has some vague memory or dream of that blessed time, the Golden Age at Mecone, when humans actually always *were* at a meal without having to do a thing about it. But any household with a woman in it will develop that insatiable, voracious hunger. In this sense the situation is similar to what occurs in beehives: On the one hand there are the worker bees, who set out early mornings for the fields, alight on all the flowers, and gather honey to carry back into the hive; and on the other hand there are the drones, who never leave home and who never get their fill either. They consume all the honey the workers have patiently gathered outside. Similarly in the human households, on one hand there are the men, who sweat over the fields, break their backs digging the furrows, tend the grain and then gather it; and on the other hand, inside the houses sit the women who—like the drones—swallow up the harvest.

Not only does she swallow up and exhaust all the resources, but that is precisely a woman's main reason for seducing a man: What she's after is the barn. Displaying the skills of her seductive talk, her deceitful cast of mind, her smiles and her "tricked-out rump," as Hesiod writes, she sings the young bachelor her big seduction aria because she actually has her eye on the grain stores. And every man—like Epimetheus before them, all agog, transfixed by her looks—every man falls captive.

Not only do women have the belly appetite that destroys a husband's health because he can never bring home enough food; they also have an enormously voracious sexual appetite. Clytemnestra, and other wives well known for betraying their husbands, always claim that they have been the watchdog (or -bitch) standing guard over the house; this bitch temperament should of course be understood in its sexual sense.

Women—even the best of them, those who are more moderate in character—all share one distinctive feature, say the Greeks: Because they were fashioned out of clay and water, their nature belongs to the world of moisture, whereas men's nature is more akin to the dry, to the warm, to fire.

In certain seasons, particularly the season called "the canicule," or "dog days"—that is, when Sirius, the Dog Star, is visible in the sky very near to the earth, when the sun and the earth are in conjunction, when it is hideously hot—men, who are dry, will tire and weaken. But women flourish because of their humid nature. They demand a level of conjugal diligence from their husbands that knocks them out.

Prometheus hatched a ruse that consisted in thieving fire from Zeus, and for that he drew a retort in the form of woman—analogous to a thieving fire—whom Zeus created to torment men. Indeed, woman, the wife, is a fire burning up her husband constantly, day after day, dessicating him and making him old before his time. Pandora is a fire that Zeus put into households and that burns men up without a flame being struck—a thieving fire in response to the theft of fire. That being the case, what should be done? If woman really were nothing more than that bitch mentality, that liar with her eye on the storehouse, with her "tricked-out rump," who is killing off her husband with age and exhaustion, then men would certainly try to manage without wives. But here again is that contrast between the inside and outside: In her animal appetite, both alimentary and sexual, woman is a *gaster*—a belly, a paunch; in a sense she represents the animality of the human species, its bestial element. As a *gaster* she devours all her husband's riches. When Prometheus wrapped the portion of food he intended for mankind in the *gaster* of the ox, he did better than he expected. There again he was caught by his own tricks. This is the dilemma now: If a man marries, his life will pretty certainly be hell, unless he happens on a very good wife, which is extremely rare. Conjugal life is thus an inferno—misery after misery. On the other hand, if a man does not marry, his life could be a happy one:

He would have his fill of everything, he would never lack for any-thing—but at his death, who will get his accumulated wealth? It will be scattered, into the hands of relatives for whom he has no particular affection. If he marries it is a catastrophe, and if he doesn't, it's another kind of catastrophe.

Woman is two different things at once: She is the paunch, the belly devouring everything her husband has laboriously gathered at the cost of his effort, his toil, his fatigue; but that belly is also the only one that can produce the thing that extends a man's life—a child. The woman's belly contradictorily represents both the dark aspect of human life, exhaustion, and also the Aphrodite aspect—the goddess who brings new births. The wife embodies both the voracity that destroys and the fecundity that produces. She is the sum of all the contradictions of our existence. Like fire, she is the emblem of the uniquely human, because only mankind marries—marriage distinguishes men from beasts, for beasts couple the way they eat, at random and by any means, so woman is the emblem of a civilized life. But at the same time, she was creat-ed in the image of the immortal goddesses: To look at a woman is to see Aphrodite, Hera, Athena. So in a sense she is also the pres-ence of the divine on this earth, in her beauty, her seductiveness, her *charis*. Woman combines the vileness of human life together with its divine aspect. She fluctuates between the gods and the beasts; that is the distinctive characteristic of humankind.

TIME GOES BY

We return to the story in a more anecdotal way. Pandora has entered Epimetheus's household; she becomes the first human wife. Zeus whispers her instructions. In this house, as in any

Greek farmer's, there are many storage jars; and among them is one particular large one, tucked away, which is never to be touched. Where did it come from? The rumor is that some satyrs brought it, but that is not certain. One day, when her husband is out, Zeus murmurs in Pandora's ear the suggestion to lift the lid off that jar and then set it right back again. This she does. She approaches the jars; there are a great many of them. Some hold wine, others grain or oil; all the food supplies are collected together there. Pandora lifts the lid of the hidden jar, and instantly all the evils, all the bad things, scatter out through the universe. When Pandora sets the lid back in place, one last thing is still left inside the jar: *elpis*—hope, expectancy for what is to come—which hadn't had time to escape.

All the evils are now out in the world through Pandora's doing. Pandora's very presence was the incarnation of all evils, and now the opened jar has made still more of them. What evils? There are myriads: fatigue, illness, death, accidents. The misfortunes are spectacularly active, moving about constantly, darting in all directions, never still. They are invisible, formless, inaudible—unlike Pandora, who is delicious to see and pleasing to hear. Zeus denied faces or voices to these evils, so that men could not guard against them or fend them off. So now the evils that men would try to avoid, because they know them to be detestable, go on lurking undetected in the world of the unseeable. The evil that can be seen and heard—woman, camouflaged by the seductive power of her beauty, her gentleness, her talk—attracts and charms you rather than rouses fear. One of the features of human existence is the dissociation between appearances—what can be seen and heard—and realities. Such is the condition of man as Zeus has concocted it in retaliation for Prometheus's tricks.

Prometheus himself doesn't fare so well, for Zeus has set him between sky and earth, halfway up a mountain and a column, and chained and tied him there. Prometheus, who had obtained for humans the mortal food that is meat, is himself now food for Zeus's bird, the eagle who carries his thunderbolt, the messenger of his invincible power. Now it is Prometheus who is the victim, a chunk of meat cut from the living flesh. Every day Zeus's eagle devours his liver completely; nothing is left of it. Overnight the liver grows back. Each day the eagle feeds on Prometheus's flesh, and each night that flesh grows back so that the eagle finds his meal intact again in the morning. So it shall be until the moment when Heracles liberates Prometheus, with Zeus's consent. (Prometheus is granted a kind of immortality in exchange for the death of the centaur Chiron. This half-divine figure—the civilizing tutor-hero who trained Achilles and so many others to be accomplished heroes—is wounded; he is in pain and his wound does not heal, but he cannot die however much he wishes it. So an exchange is negotiated: Chiron is granted death, and his immortality is passed on to Prometheus. Both are set free.)

Prometheus's punishment was made to fit his crime. He determined to give mortals meat, especially the liver—a choice morsel from a sacrificed animal because the liver is the organ that diviners examine to see whether the gods accept a sacrifice. Now in turn, by his liver Prometheus becomes the favorite food of Zeus's eagle. That eagle is a symbol of the divine thunder; he is the fire bearer for Zeus the thunderer. In a way the fire that Prometheus stole is turning on his own liver, slicing off an ever-replenished meal for itself.

And there is another detail of some significance. Prometheus is an ambiguous being; his position in the divine world is not clear. The story of that liver devoured every day and regrown exactly the same overnight demonstrates that there are at least three types of time and of life energy. There is the gods' time: eternity, where nothing happens and everything is already present, nothing disappears. There is man's time: linear, always moving in the same direction: A person is born, grows up, is adult, grows old, and dies. All living things are subject to that rule; as Plato says, it is a kind of time that proceeds in a straight line. And finally there is a third type of time, one that Prometheus's liver brings to mind: a circular or zigzag time. It describes an existence like the moon's, for instance, which grows large, and dies, and is reborn, and repeats the cycle endlessly. This Promethean time is like the movements of the stars—that is, like those circular movements traced out in time and providing a measure for time. It's not the gods' eternity; nor is it terrestrial, mortal time, always moving in the same direction. It is a time philosophers can describe as "the mobile image of immobile eternity." As character, too, Prometheus is strung like his liver between humans' linear time and the eternal being of the gods. His function as mediator in this story emerges very clearly. He is even positioned between sky and earth, midway up on a column, betwixt and between. He represents the transition between that very remote era when the cosmos was already organized but there was as yet no time, when gods and men lived mingled together, when nondeath—immortality—reigned; and the era of mortals, henceforward to be separate from the gods, subject to death and to the passage of time. Prometheus's liver is like the stars—a thing that imparts rhythm and measure to the gods' eternity and that also mediates between the divine world and the human.

The Trojan War

To tell the story of the Trojan War again after the poet who brought it to us, Homer—well, why bother? It could only be a poor summary. But what one might do is try to set out in narrative form the reasons for, and the meaning of, the conflict. Its roots stretch back into a very ancient past. To try to understand, we travel to several mountains that figure in the beginnings of this drama lived out by mortals. There is Mount Pelion, in Greece; there is Mount Ida, in Trojan territory; and there is Mount Taygetus at Sparta. These are very high peaks—that is, places where the distance between the gods and humans is less than it is elsewhere; where the frontiers between mortals and immortals, while not entirely absent, do become somewhat porous. Occasionally there is some slippage between what is divine and what is human. Sometimes—and this is the case with the Trojan War—the gods make use of that proximity, of those encounters up on the peaks, to pass along to humans the misfortunes and catastrophes they want to shed, expelling them from the shining realm where they have set up headquarters and setting them down onto the earth's surface.

So it all begins on Mount Pelion, with the wedding of King Peleus of Phthia to the nereid Thetis. Like her fifty sister sea nymphs, who populate the surface waters and the ocean deeps with their propitious and lovely presence, Thetis is the daughter of Nereus, known as the Old Man of the Sea. Nereus is himself a son of Pontus—Sea—whom Gaia produced at the same time she did Uranus, Sky, at the beginning of the universe. Through their mother, Doris, the nereids are descended from Oceanus, the primordial cosmic river, who girdles the universe and grips it within the circular network of his waters. Together with Amphitryon, Thetis is perhaps one of the most representative of the nereids. Like other sea goddesses, she has a spectacular gift for metamorphosis. She can take any form—she can turn into a lion, a flame, a palm tree or bird or fish. She has a vast repertory of transformations. Being a sea goddess, she is utter fluidity, as water is; no form binds her. She can shift constantly from one look to another, escape her own appearance like water flowing away between the fingers, impossible to hold. That goddess—perhaps just because of that extreme suppleness, that ungraspable fluidity—represents for the Greeks a kind of power that only a few deities were granted when prerogatives were being doled out—for instance, the one whom Zeus married the first time around, the goddess Metis.

As we have seen, Zeus did not merely wed Metis as he did other goddesses; he also made her his first consort, because he knew that for the very reason of her extraordinary qualities of suppleness, subtlety, fluid style, a child that Metis should bear him would turn out to be cleverer and more powerful than he. That is why no sooner does he make the goddess pregnant than by trickery, he swallows her down and absorbs her into himself. The forthcoming offspring will be Athena, and there will be no others. Metis's subtle, undulating power is now entirely enclosed in Zeus's body. And therefore there will never be a son to conquer his father when the time comes. This is opposite to the customary lot of humans: However strong a man may be, however powerful, intelligent, regal, and sovereign, the day comes when time does him in, when age weighs him down, and when, consequently, the offspring he created, the little tyke he used to bounce on his knee and protect and nourish becomes a man who is stronger than his father and is destined to take his place. But in the world of the gods, once Zeus is enthroned and established, nothing and no one can set him aside and sit on his throne.

As to Thetis: With her gift, her magic for metamorphosis, she is a ravishing creature, deeply seductive. Two major gods are enamored of her: Zeus and Poseidon. They are vying for her, and each of them expects to marry her. In Zeus's conflict with Prometheus within the world of the gods, one weapon Prometheus holds in reserve—a card he can play—is that he and he alone knows a dreadful secret about this Thetis business: that a child of Thetis is destined to overthrow his father. So if Zeus gets his wish, if he does succeed in mating with her, their child will one day inflict on him what Zeus himself inflicted on his father, Cronus; and Cronus on his father, Uranus. The war of the generations—the rivalry that sets young against old, father against son—would enter the world of the gods for all time, and would endlessly call into question the system Zeus intended to be immutable, the way he established it in his position as sovereign of the universe.

How does Zeus manage to learn Prometheus's secret? One story tells that the two come to some reconciliation, and that the king of the gods authorizes Heracles to free the Titan on condition that he reveal the secret. Zeus is thus forewarned of the danger, and so is Poseidon. Both gods renounce the idea of union with Thetis. So must she remain a virgin forever, and never know love? No, the gods are magnanimous; they will unload onto mankind the fateful truth that, when the time comes, one must step aside for the young. Thetis does later bear a mortal child who is in every regard extraordinary, and who does surpass his father in every realm: a model hero who represents the very pinnacle of warrior virtues in the human world. He will be the best, matchless. Who is that child to be? Thetis's son by Peleus, Achilles. He is one of the major figures of the Trojan War, whose very outbreak is bound up in this whole affair.

PELEUS'S MARRIAGE

So Zeus and the other gods determine unilaterally that the Thessalean Peleus, king of Phthia, shall marry Thetis. How will they get the goddess to agree? How to convince her that she must lower herself and marry what is a mere mortal, even though a king? The gods have no right to interfere with one of their kind and order such a misalliance. Peleus will have to manage on his own to win this wife; he will have to do as other heroes have done to conquer a sea god and obtain what they hope from her. (Menelaus had contended with Proteus and his transformations to wrest a secret from him.) Peleus will have to abduct Thetis and, as the ritual requires, carry her away from her dwelling place in the sea to his mansion—the palace, the hearth and home of her future husband.

And so Peleus turns up one fine day at the edge of the sea. He sees Thetis rise from the waves, he speaks to her, he seizes her by the arm and draws her to him. To escape him she turns herself into every shape there is. Peleus has been warned: With these fluctuating, metamorphizing deities, the only way to proceed is to imprison them in an unyielding grip, a grip that wraps right around them. He must enclose the goddess in the encircling bond of his arms, his two hands welded tight to each other, no matter what form she takes—a boar, a lion, a scorching flame, water—and not let go whatever happens. Then the vanquished goddess will quit deploying the full array of shapes available to her. And that has its limits; when she has run through the whole cycle of borrowed appearances, she returns to her original, true form—that of a young and beautiful goddess: She is defeated.

The last form Thetis takes in her effort to get free from the binding embrace is that of a cuttlefish. Ever after, the narrow spit of land where this prenuptial struggle took place is called "Cape Sepias"—Cuttlefish Cape. Why a cuttlefish? Because, when someone tries to catch it, or when some ocean predator threatens it, the cuttlefish will stain the water around it with the black ink that completely conceals the animal; it vanishes, as if drowned, in a blackness produced and disseminated by its own doing. This is Thetis's last resort; like the cuttlefish she must eject her ink. But even enveloped in that general blackness, Peleus hangs on; he does not loosen his grip, and finally Thetis is forced to surrender. The marriage will indeed take place.

And it is celebrated on the very peak of Pelion. It is not only a mountain that draws the gods closer to men, that brings them together at the end of an unequal exchange. It is also that, through this privilege of marriage to a goddess, the gods are sending over to Peleus all the perils that such a marriage involves for immortals—which they want none of, which they must somehow manage to pass off onto the human world. All the gods foregather; they come down from Olympus, from the shining heavens, onto Pelion's peaks. There the marriage is celebrated.

The mountain is more than a meeting-point between gods and humans; it is also an ambiguous place: the realm of the centaurs, and in particular of the centaur Chiron, the oldest, most illustrious of them all. The centaurs have an ambivalent status, an ambiguous position. They have the head of a man, somewhat horselike forequarters, and then a horse's body: They are wild creatures, both subhuman and cruel—they are capable of drunkenness, of rape. But they are also superhuman; like Chiron they represent a model of wisdom, of courage, of all the virtues a young man must develop to become a truly heroic figure: He must hunt, be skilled with every weapon, sing, dance, debate, maintain self-control. These are the lessons the centaur Chiron teaches many boys, and Achilles in particular. And it is here—in this place where the gods and men mingle, where creatures at once bestial and superhuman live—that the marriage is held.

The Muses sing the wedding hymn, the epithalamium; all the gods bring gifts. Peleus, the bridegroom, is given an ashwood spear, a suit of armor forged by Hephaestus himself, and two marvelous and immortal steeds: Balius and Zanthos. Nothing can overtake these two; they are as swift as the wind, and sometimes they speak instead of whinnying: At special moments, when men's doom, as commanded by the gods, looms on the battlefield, they reveal themselves as endowed with human voice, and utter prophetic words as if the faraway gods were speaking through them, right at hand. In the combat between Achilles and Hector, after Hector's defeat and death the horses speak to Achilles to tell him that soon he too will die.

Amid the joy, the singing and dancing, amid the gods' display of largess to Peleus on the occasion of his marriage, there appears on Mount Pelion an uninvited guest: the goddess Eris—discord, jealousy, hatred. She barges into the very midst of the feasting, and although unsummoned, she brings a magnificent love gift: a golden apple, a token of the passion felt for a beloved. With all the gods gathered and feasting, with the other gifts on display, Eris tosses the marvelous present into the center of the feast. But the fruit bears an inscription, a motto: For the Loveliest. There are three goddesses there—Athena, Hera, Aphrodite—each of them fully convinced that the apple should rightfully go to her. Which will carry off the fruit?

That golden apple, that marvelous gleaming, glittering jewel, lies there on the peak of Pelion, waiting for someone to take it up. Gods and men are assembled for the wedding—despite all of Thetis's magic spells, Peleus has managed to capture her—and then appears that apple, which starts the Trojan War.

The roots of the war are located not only in the random ways of human history; they arise from a far more complex situation having to do with the nature of relations between the gods and men. Because the gods want to avoid aging and the struggle between succeeding generations, they hand such troubles on to men at the same time as they give men goddesses for wives. So the tragic situation arises: Men cannot celebrate rites of marriage without experiencing rites of death as well. At the heart of marriage, in the pact between beings so different as men and women, stand linked together Ares— the god of war, who severs, who sets at odds—and Aphrodite, who makes peace and brings unity. Love, passion, seduction, erotic pleasure are in a sense the other face of that violence, of the desire to conquer the adversary. But while the union of the sexes does provide for the renewal of the generations, while mankind reproduces, while these marriages do repopulate the earth, the tradeoff is that the numbers grow too great.

When the Greeks themselves reflect on the Trojan War, they sometimes say that its true cause was that the massive increase in population; the gods grew exasperated with the noisy mob and decided to purge them from the earth's surface—as in the Babylonian tales in which the gods decide to send down the deluge. Men make too much racket. There is the ethereal, silent realm where the gods withdraw to think and gaze upon one another, and then there are these humans, jumping about and agitating, shouting themselves hoarse with quarreling. So from the gods' standpoint, a good war every now and then solves the problem: back to peace and quiet.

THREE GODDESSES AND A GOLDEN APPLE

Thus ends the first act of the scenario leading to the Trojan War. Who will get the apple—the award for beauty among the deities? The gods cannot come to a decision. If Zeus were to choose, only one single goddess would be gratified at the expense of the two others. As an impartial ruler, he has already laid out the powers, the territories, the relative privileges of each of the three goddesses. If Zeus picks Hera, he will be accused of partiality toward his wife; if he chooses Athena, he will be accused of paternal bias, and if he declares for Aphrodite it will prove he's easy prey to erotic desire. Nothing in the protocol of precedences among them can be changed. It is impossible for him to make the award. Here again an ordinary mortal will have to take over the task. Here again the gods shift over to men the responsibility for decisions they shy from, the same way they sent them the misfortunes or baleful fates they wanted to avoid for themselves.

Second act. Setting: Mount Ida. This is where the young men come to train in heroism. Like Mount Pelion it is a realm of high, open wilderness, far from cities, from cultivated fields and vineyards and orchards; a terrain of harsh, rustic life; of solitude, with no other company but shepherds and their flocks; of the hunt for wild beasts. A youth, still half wild himself, comes here to apprentice in the virtues of courage, endurance, and mastery that go to make the heroic man.

The person selected to decide the competition among the three goddesses is named Paris. Paris is the youngest son of Priam, king of Troy, that great Asian city on the coast of Anatolia—a very rich, very beautiful, very powerful city. When Hermes, with the three goddesses behind him, comes down to Mount Ida to ask Paris to arbitrate and say which he thinks the loveliest, the youth is watching over his father's royal herds on the slopes. He is a kind of shepherd king or royal shepherd, then—very young, a *kouros*, still in the bloom of adolescence.

Paris has had an extraordinary childhood and youth: Just before his birth, Queen Hecuba dreamed she was bringing forth not a human creature but a torch that would set fire to the city of Troy. Naturally she asked a soothsayer, or some kinsmen known for their skill at interpreting dreams, what that meant. She was given a somewhat obvious answer: that this child would be the death of Troy, its destruction by fire and flame. What to do? What the ancients always did in such cases: arrange for the infant to die without exactly killing him: Expose him to the elements. Priam entrusts the child to a shepherd with instructions to abandon him, without food, without care, without protection, in those same lonely realms where the young heroes trained—not on the cultivated, settled plain but on the harsh flanks of that mountain remote from humans and overrun by wild beasts. To expose a child is to send him to death without soiling one's hands with his blood, dispatch him to the beyond, make him disappear. But it sometimes happens that the child does not die. When by some chance he reappears, he returns with qualities that arise from the very fact that, having been put out to die, he has undergone that hardship and survived it. Having passed at birth through the portals of death, and victoriously, does confer on the escapee the gleam of someone exceptional, someone elect. What happened in Paris's case? It is said that a female bear nursed him for the first several days. Because of the way they walk and care for their young, female bears are often seen as a kind of humanlike mother. This particular bear nurses the newborn Paris for a short while, and then some herdsmen guarding the king's cattle on Mount Ida come across him and take him in. They raise him in their midst without knowing, of course, who he is. They call him Alexander rather than Paris, the name his mother and father gave him at birth.

The years go by. One day an emissary from the palace comes to select the finest bull from the royal herd for a funerary sacrifice that Priam and Hecuba are planning to offer in memory of the child they sent to death, to honor the child from whom they were obliged to separate. The bull he chooses is the favorite of the young Alexander, who decides to go along with it and try to save its life. As always at such memorial ceremonies, there are not only sacrifices but also games and contests—footraces, boxing, wrestling, javelin throwing. Young Alexander signs up to compete against Priam's other sons, against the elite of Troy's young men. He wins all the matches.

Everyone is stunned and curious to learn about this unknown young herdsman, so fine to see, so strong, so skilled. Priam's son Deiphobus—we will hear more of him in the course of this story—is seized with rage, and he determines to kill this intruder who has bested them all. He pursues young Alexander, who takes refuge in the temple of Zeus. There in the temple is their sister, Cassandra, a very beautiful young virgin whom Apollo loved but who rejected him. To retaliate he granted her an infallible gift for prophecy, but he made it useless to her—in fact it only worsens her misfortune: No one ever believes her predictions. In the present situation she announces: "Hear me—this stranger is our little brother Paris!" Indeed, Paris/Alexander does display the swaddling clothes he wore when he was exposed on the hillside, and he is instantly recognized. His mother, Hecuba, is wild with joy, and Priam, a very good old king, is delighted to recover his son. Paris rejoins the royal family.

Zeus has charged Hermes with settling the apple award problem, and by the time Hermes brings the three goddesses to see Paris about it, the boy has already resumed his place in the household. Since he spent his whole youth as a herdsman, though, he still keeps up his custom of visiting the flocks; he is a Mount Ida man. So: Paris sees Hermes and the three goddesses approaching him on the mountain, and he is somewhat startled and uneasy. Uneasy because when a goddess openly shows herself nude to a human, in her true nature as an immortal, matters tend to go badly for the former: A mortal is not entitled to look upon divinity. It is both an extraordinary privilege and a danger from which one does not recover. The Theban prophet Tiresias, for instance, lost his sight from having looked upon Athena. And right here on Mount Ida, Aphrodite descended from heaven and coupled with Anchises: The child Aeneas would be born of their union. After sleeping with her as if she were an ordinary mortal, the next morning Anchises sees her in all her divine beauty, and he is terrified. He implores her, "I know I am lost—I can never again have carnal contact with a woman. A man who has coupled with a goddess will never lie in the arms of a mere mortal again. His life, his eyes, and certainly his virility are destroyed."

To start with, then, Paris is frightened. Hermes reassures him. He tells Paris he must select the winner, must award the prize—so the gods have decided—and that it is up to him to judge, to declare which goddess he thinks the loveliest. Paris feels extremely awkward. All three goddesses, probably of equal beauty, try to sway him with tantalizing promises. Each swears, if he chooses her, to endow him with some unique, extraordinary power that she alone can grant.

What can Athena offer? She tells him: "If you choose me, you shall have victory in your every battle and wisdom the whole world will envy." Hera declares, "If you choose me, you will have a throne; you will rule over the whole of Asia, for the bed of the wife of Zeus is the source of sovereignty." As for Aphrodite, she announces: "If you pick me, you will be the compleat seducer; the finest women will be yours, and in particular, the lovely Helen, the woman already renowned the world over. When that woman lays eyes on you she will not resist you. You will be the lover, and the husband, of the lovely Helen." Victory in war, or kingship, or the lovely Helen—beauty, pleasure, happiness with a woman . . . Paris chooses for Helen, and awards the apple to Aphrodite. And, given the background of knotty relations between men and the gods, that choice instantly activates the machinery whose workings constitute the second act of this story.

HELEN—GUILTY OR INNOCENT?

The third act turns around Helen. Who is Helen? She is herself the fruit of the gods' intrusion into the human world. Her mother, Leda, a mortal, is the daughter of Thestius, the king of Calydon. When she is very young Leda meets Tyndareus, a Lacedaemonian from Sparta, driven from his country by the winds of political life, who has found refuge with Thestius. Before returning home to recover the kingly rank that was stripped from him, Tyndareus falls in love with Leda and asks her hand in marriage. The wedding is celebrated with great pomp. But the girl's extraordinary beauty has attracted others besides her husband: Zeus has spotted her from the heights of Olympus. With no regard for Hera or any other of his goddess wives, he has gotten a single idea into his head: making love to that young woman. The day of the marriage, on the very night Tyndareus and Leda first share a bed, Zeus joins her there and couples with her too, in the guise of a swan. Leda carries the children of both Tyndareus and Zeus in her womb at the same time—four of them: two girls, two boys.

Some versions say it was actually a goddess, Nemesis, whom Zeus raped: that she had turned into a goose to elude him, and that Zeus had made himself a swan to cover her. The scene was supposed to have occurred high on Mount Taygetus, near Sparta, and there on its peak, says this version, the goose/Nemesis lays her egg (or two eggs), which a herdsman rushes off to Queen Leda. At the palace the infants hatch from their shells, and Leda adopts them as her own.

Nemesis is a fearsome deity, a daughter out of Night, fathered by gloom, as were her brothers and sisters: Death, the Fates, and Strife (Eris) with her attendants—Murders, Slaughters, Battles. But Nemesis also contains the other aspects of feminine darkness: Sweet Lies (Pseudea) and Erotic Attachment (Philotes), which mixes pleasures and betrayals. Nemesis is an avenger who sees to retaliation for crimes; she never rests till she has caught the culprit to punish him, till she has brought down the upstart who climbed too high and provoked the gods to jealousy by his overweening success. Nemesis/Leda: It is as if Nemesis the goddess takes on the guise of Leda, a mere human, to make mortals pay for the misfortune of not being gods.

So, then: four offspring—two boys, Castor and Pollux (the Dioscuri, the "children of Zeus," who are also the Tyndarides, or children of Tyndareus); and two girls, Helen and Clytemnestra. In them are combined—for better or worse—the divine and the human: the seed of Tyndareus the human/husband mingling with that of Zeus the god/lover within Nemesis/Leda's womb, to be linked together yet still distinct and opposite. Of the male twins, Pollux comes straight from Zeus, and he is immortal; Castor has more of Tyndareus, and is mortal. In a battle against their two cousins, Idas and Lynceus, Castor is killed and descends to Hades, while Pollux, victorious but wounded, Zeus elevates in glory to Mount Olympus. Yet despite their differing ancestry and their contrasting natures, the twin brothers remain twins so tightly bound, so inseparable, that in Sparta they are symbolized by a pair of parallel beams bracketed together—in wartime the device is carried into battle. Zeus grants Pollux's plea to share his own immortality equally with his brother, each of them to stay half the time in heaven with the gods and the other half underground in Hades, in the kingdom of the shades, with the mortals. Clytemnestra and Helen also go together, as a double calamity. But Clytemnestra, who is said to be Tyndareus's entirely human daughter, is pitch dark: She embodies the curse that weighs on the House of Atreus; she is the avenging spirit who brings a shameful death down on the conqueror of Troy, her husband, Agamemnon.

Helen, however, is Zeus's daughter, and she retains an aura of the divine even in the disasters she brings on. Her dazzling beauty, though its seductive power makes her a terrifying figure, never ceases to shine from her person and halo her in a light that shimmers with the divine. When she abandons her husband, her palace, her children to follow after a young foreigner proposing an adulterous affair, is she guilty? Is she innocent? By some accounts she succumbed quite readily to the call of desire, to sensual delight, out of her fascination with the luxury, the wealth, the opulence, the Eastern splendor of the foreign prince. Other accounts claim the contrary: that she was abducted by force, against her will and despite her resistance.

One thing is certain, though: Helen's flight with Paris set off the Trojan War. However, that war would not have been what it was if the only issue were the jealousy of a husband determined to take back his wife. The matter is much graver, a clash of opposing poles: Peace, hospitality, neighborly bonds, and commitments come up against violence, hatred, wrenching ruptures. Years earlier, when Helen reached marriageable age, her father—faced with such beauty, so precious a jewel—realized that choosing a husband for her was no small matter. He therefore sent out a call for all the youths and princes and bachelor kings in Greece to gather at his palace for a selection to be made openly among them. They stay for some time at the king's court. What shall he decide? Tyndareus is at a loss. He calls on a very shrewd nephew, Odysseus, whom we mention because he also plays a role in this story. Odysseus tells Helen's father something like: "There's only one thing you can do. Before making your choice, which will certainly set off some rumbling, you get all the suitors to vow, unanimously, that whatever Helen decides, they will abide by her choice; and that furthermore they will all commit themselves to this marriage. If the man she chooses should run into some problem in his marital situation, they will stand behind him." They all swear to the oath, and then ask Helen to declare her choice. She names Menelaus, king of Sparta.

Menelaus already knew Paris; on his journey through Trojan territory the young prince had been his host. Now, when in turn Paris visits Greece with Aeneas, he is first received with great ceremony by Helen's brothers, Castor and Pollux, and then Menelaus brings him to Sparta, where Helen is in residence. For a time Menelaus is there to shower his guest with gifts and attentions, but then he is called away to a kinsman's funeral. He passes Helen his duties as host. It is that funeral and Menelaus's absence that bring Helen to welcome the guest more personally. With Menelaus present, the women of the royal palace of Sparta probably did not associate closely with an outsider; that was the king's task. Now it is Helen's.

Paris and Aeneas board ship again and head straight for Troy with the lovely Helen—consenting or constrained—in the hold. After returning to Sparta, Menelaus rushes to his brother, Agamemnon, to bring word of Helen's betrayal, and above all of Paris's treachery. Agamemnon orders a number of men, Odysseus among them, to go around to all the former suitors and muster support. The offense is such that, even apart from Menelaus and Agamemnon, all of Greece must rally to punish Paris for the abduction of a woman who is not only lovely beyond compare but a Greek, a wife, a queen. In affairs of honor, though, negotiation can precede—and sometimes replace—armed conflict. So first Menelaus and Odysseus set off on a mission to Troy to seek an amicable settlement—to restore harmony and hospitality, perhaps through the payment of some fine or other reparation for the wrong. They are received in Troy. Some prominent Trojans favor this peaceable solution—one is the Greeks' host, Deiphobus, a son of Priam. But the decision lies with Troy's assembly of elders; this business is beyond even the king's power. The two Greeks are therefore received in the assembly chamber, where some other members of Priam's family not only scheme against any compromise but even suggest that Odysseus and Menelaus should not be allowed to leave the place alive. But as guests of Deiphobus, they are under his protection. They return to Greece empty-handed, and announce the failure of the conciliation effort. Everything is set for the outbreak of the conflict.

DIE YOUNG, LIVE ON IN GLORY

The expedition against Troy seems not, at the outset, to have roused wholehearted enthusiasm among the Greeks. Even Odysseus hoped to avoid involvement. Penelope had just borne him a son, Telemachus, and he felt it was a poor time to abandon the mother and child. Told of the project to set sail and take the stolen Helen back by force of arms, he tries to evade the obligation by feigning insanity—the soundest, canniest man in the world starts behaving like a halfwit. The aged chieftain Nestor has come all the way to Ithaca to bring him the mustering orders. He finds Odysseus pulling a plow hitched to a donkey and an ox; the hero is stepping along backward and sowing pebbles instead of grain. Everyone is horrified at the sight—everyone but Nestor, who is sharp enough to guess that Odysseus is pulling one of his tricks. As Odysseus moves along backward and the cart advances, Nestor seizes baby Telemachus and sets him down in the path of the plowshare. Odysseus promptly recovers his senses and snatches the child up out of harm's way. He is thus unmasked, and he agrees to go to fight.

Old Peleus, Thetis's husband, has seen several of his children die; he has only Achilles left, and he cannot bear the idea that the boy might some day go off to war. He therefore sends the young boy to stay on the island of Skyros, among the daughters of the local king. Achilles lives there as a girl in their *gynaeceum*, the women's quarters. He had spent his childhood being raised by Chiron and the centaurs; now he is reaching the age when the sexes do not yet show particular signs, are not fully differentiated. His beard has not yet sprouted, he has no body hair, he looks like a pretty little girl—with that indeterminate beauty of adolescents who might as easily be girls as boys, boys as girls. He dwells carefree among his pretty companions. Odysseus comes to fetch him, but is told that there are no boys in the place. Disguised as a wandering peddler with his wares, Odysseus asks permission to enter the women's quarters. He sees some fifty girls there; Achilles does not stand out among them. Odysseus opens his sack and displays cloth and needlework, clips and jewels, and forty-nine of the girls crowd around to exclaim over his trinkets. But one of them hangs back, indifferent. Odysseus then takes out a dagger, and that pretty little girl lunges for it. Outside the walls a battle trumpet blares: panic in the women's quarters, the forty-nine girls dart away with their bits of frippery, while just one—with dagger in hand—heads for the marching music. Odysseus has unmasked Achilles just as Nestor unmasked Odysseus—and Achilles in turn is ready to go to war.

With all the children Thetis bore Peleus before Achilles—seven boys—the goddess could not accept their status as mere mortals like their father. So from the first she schemed to turn them immortal. She lay each of them into fire, to scorch away the rot-promoting dampness that keeps humans from being pure blazing flame; but in the fire every son burned and died. Poor Peleus was devastated. So when Achilles was born, Peleus determined to save this one at least. Now, as the mother prepared to lay the child in the fire, the father stepped in and snatched him away. The fire touched only his lips and one bone in his heel; the heel died. Peleus asked the centaur Chiron to go to Mount Pelion and dig up the buried cadaver of a centaur who in life had been an extremely swift runner, to take a heel from the corpse and set it into place on young Achilles. From his earliest childhood, then, Achilles could run as swiftly as a stag. That is one version. Another tells that in her quest to make him immortal, when Thetis was stopped from thrusting him into fire she thrust him instead into the Styx, the underworld river that separates the living from the dead. Of course, any person who is plunged into the waters of the Styx and comes out alive has gained extraordinary capacities and resources. Achilles was immersed in those infernal waters and he survived the ordeal; only the heel by which his mother dangled him missed contact with the water. So now Achilles is not just the swift-running warrior; he is also a soldier invulnerable to human wounds except at his heel, the one spot where death can steal in.

One result of his parents' unequal marriage between goddess and human is that some of the splendor, the power, of the divine Thetis comes to glow around Achilles. At the same time he is a tragic fig-ure: not a god, yet unable to live or to die like an ordinary man, as a simple mortal; but escaping mankind's common condition does not make him a divine being guaranteed eternal life. His fate stands as a model for every warrior, every Greek of the time, and it con-tinues to fascinate us even now: It rouses us by its echo to an aware-ness of what makes human existence—limited, torn, divided—a drama in which light and shadow, joy and sorrow, life and death are inextricably tangled together.   Achilles' fate is exemplary; it is marked with the seal of ambiguity. By birth half human and half divine, he cannot belong entirely to one or the other.

At the brink of his life, with his very first steps, the road before him forks. Whichever direction he chooses, to follow it he must deny an essential part of himself. He cannot rejoice in what to humans is sweet-est about life in the sunlight and also have the privilege of never losing it—of not dying. Rejoicing in life—in that possession most precious to ephemeral creatures, that unique possession that, unlike any other because it is the only one that once lost cannot be recovered—means giving up any hope of immortality. To wish oneself immortal is, in part, to agree to lose life even before having fully lived it. If Achilles chooses—as his aged father hopes—to stay put at home in Phthia among family and in safety, he will have a long, peaceful, happy life, coursing through the whole cycle of the time granted to mortals into an old age surrounded with affection. But, however fine it might be, even brightened by the best fortune a man's career on this earth can bring, his existence will leave no trace of its light behind it: When it is done that life decays in darkness, in nothingness. The hero disappears with the life, entirely and forever. Plunging down into Hades, without name, without face, without memory, he vanishes as if he had never existed.

Or else Achilles may take the other option: a short life and everlasting glory. He chooses to go off to distant places, leave everything behind, risk all, hand himself over—pledge himself to death from the start. He wants to count among the small number of the elect who care not for comfort, or riches, or commonplace honors, but who want to win battles where the stake each time is their very life. To face in combat the sharpest, most seasoned adversaries is to prove oneself in a contest of valor where each man must show what he is, demonstrate for all eyes his excellence, an excellence that reaches its peak in battle and finds its completion in a "fine death." In the full flush of combat, of youth, the manly strengths of bravura and energy and youthful grace intact will thus never know the decrepitude of old age.

As if, in order to shine in its purest splendor, the flame of life must be brought to such a pitch of incandescence that it burns to ash at the very instant it is kindled. Achilles chooses death with glory, in the everlasting beauty of a very young life. A life cut short, amputated, shrunken—and undying glory. Achilles' name, his adventures, his history, his person will live forever in the memory of men, generations of them filing by, century upon century, vanishing one after another into the obscurity and silence of death.

Odysseus:
The Human Adventure

The Greeks are victorious. After so many years of siege and warfare at the walls of Troy, the city has fallen at last. The Greeks did not stop at conquering it, taking it; they sacked it and burned it, by means of a trick—the well-known wooden horse the Trojans drew into their city believing it was a pious offering to the gods. A squad of Greek scouts emerged from the horse's flanks, opened the city gates from the inside, and let the Greek army in to overrun the city and massacre everything in its path. The men were killed, the women and children carried off as slaves; there is nothing left but ruins. The Greeks believe that the matter is finally settled, but then the other face of this great military adventure comes to light. One way or another, the Greeks are going to have to pay for their crimes, their excesses, their *hubris* in the very course of winning.

From the start disagreement rumbles between Agamemnon and Menelaus. The latter hopes to leave immediately and get right home; Agamemnon, though, wants to stay on and make a sacrifice to Athena, who supported the Greeks' cause among the gods and thus determined their victory. With the twelve vessels he had brought to Troy, Odysseus decides to set off immediately for Ithaca. He embarks with Menelaus on the same ship that is also carrying old Nestor. But then, at the isle of Tenedos, Odysseus has a falling-out with Menelaus, and he turns back to Troy to rejoin Agamemnon there. They plan to sail in convoy in the hope of reaching continental Greece at the same time. The gods decide otherwise. Gales and storms and tempest burst over them. The flotilla scatters; a number of ships sink, taking down their crews of seamen and soldiers. Few Greeks are lucky enough to return to their own homes. And among those the sea spares, some will meet death on their very doorstep. (Agamemnon is one such: Barely has he set foot on his native soil than he falls into the snare set for him by his wife Clytemnestra and Aegisthus, this faithless wife's lover. Agamemnon, all unsuspecting, was just coming home like a good ox pleased to get back to the old familiar barn. He is ruthlessly struck down and slaughtered by the two conspirators.)

So then: The tempest separated Agamemnon's ships, the larger part of the fleet, from those of Odysseus, and Odysseus is alone on the seas with his own flotilla. He faces the same ordeals, weathers the same storms as his comrades in distress. When at last he disembarks in Thrace among the Cicones, the reception is hostile. Odysseus seizes their city, Ismaros. He behaves toward the vanquished as did many Greek heroes: He kills most of the city's inhabitants. But he does spare one: Maron, the priest of Apollo. In thanks Maron offers him several goatskins full of a wine that is no ordinary drink but a kind of divine nectar. Odysseus has the wineskins stored on his ships. The Greeks are pleased, and they set up camp for the night along the shore, expecting to sail on at break of day. But the Cicones from the countryside are alerted to the enemy presence; they attack them at dawn and kill a great many. The survivors clamber hastily onto the ships, cast off, and flee as fast as they can.

IN THE COUNTRY OF FORGETTING

And so they sail on, the fleet much reduced. A little farther along, Odysseus approaches Cape Malea and passes it. From that point he can already sight the shores of Ithaca, his homeland. He feels as if he is home again. But just as he imagines his trip is over, the curtain rises on another part of Odysseus's journey: All he had done so far was the voyage of any naval commander heading back from a military expedition across the sea. When they round Cape Malea, though, a tempest suddenly crashes down on the Greeks. It will blow for seven long days, moving the flotilla into a region utterly different from the one in which it had been sailing. Odysseus has no idea where he is; from now on he will meet no one like the Cicones, hostile warriors but still people similar to himself. In a way he leaves the bounds of the known world, of the human *oikoumenos*, and enters a realm of nonhumankind, a world of elsewhere.

From this point on Odysseus comes across only beings who are either quasi divine, who feed on nectar and ambrosia, like Circe or Calypso, or beings who are subhuman, monsters like the Cyclopes or the Laestrygonians, cannibals who feed on human flesh. For the Greeks the signal feature of man—what defines him as such—is the fact of eating bread and drinking wine, having a certain kind of food and acknowledging the laws of hospitality, welcoming the foreigner rather than devouring him. The universe into which Odysseus and his sailors have been thrown by the terrible tempest is the complete opposite of this normal human world. Scarcely has the tempest abated when the Greeks make out a shoreline; they land in an unknown country. To learn something about who lives there, and to find provisions, Odysseus picks a few sailors and sends them off as scouts, as an advance party, to make contact with the local people. They are received with enormous kindness. The natives are full of smiles, and they invite the foreign seamen to share their usual meal. Now, the inhabitants of this country are the Lotophagi—the lotus eaters. Just as man feeds on bread and wine, so they eat an exquisite plant, the lotus. If a human should consume that delicious food, he forgets everything. He no longer recalls his own past, he loses all notion of who he is, where he comes from, where he's going. Anyone who eats of the lotus ceases to live as men live, with the memory of the past in them and the sense of what they are.

When they meet their companions again, Odysseus's scouts refuse to go back to sea and they are incapable of telling what's happened to them. They seem drugged, in a sort of bliss that paralyzes all remembrance. All they ask is to stay right where they are, as they are, with no more connections and no past, no expectations, no yearning for home. Odysseus takes them by the nape of the neck, sets them squarely on their ships, and sails off. So that was the first stop: a land that is the country of forgetting.

Throughout the long journey to follow, at every moment, behind all Odysseus's adventures with his companions, this forgetting—the erasure of any memory of the homeland, any desire to return to it—forgetting is the constant danger, the evil. To be in the human world is to be living in sunlight, seeing other people and being seen by them, living in mutuality, bearing in mind both oneself and other people. Here, though, they are entering a world where nocturnal powers—the children of Night, as Hesiod calls them—will slowly spread their sinister shadow over Odysseus's crew and over Odysseus himself. A cloud of darkness hangs perpetually over the navigators, and it threatens to be their undoing if they fall to forgetting about the journey home.

ODYSSEUS HIMSELF FACES CYCLOPS

They have left the island of the lotus eaters. Odysseus's ship sails on, and then the flotilla is overwhelmed by some kind of fog; nothing can be seen. It is evening; the ship moves along under its own power; the sailors need neither row or see ahead. Suddenly they run aground on an island they had not noticed; they can make out nothing. The sea itself or the gods have pushed the ship toward this invisible island where they touch shore in utter darkness. Even the moon is absent. They cannot make out a thing. They're simply here, with no forewarning of what is befalling them. It is as if, after that island of forgetting, the portal of darkness—of night—were yawning open before them, a corridor where they will encounter some new adventures. They step out onto land. This little isle looks across a narrow bay to a highland, the promontory home of those monstrous giants with a single eye in the middle of the forehead, who are called the Cyclopes.

Odysseus pulls his ship to shelter in a creek and climbs with a dozen men to the top of the hill, where he has spotted a cavern and where he hopes to find provisions. The party enters that enormous cave, and there they see loaded cheese racks and signs of significant farming activity. There are no cereals, but there are flocks of livestock, and the cheeses, and perhaps even some wild grapes lower down. Naturally Odysseus's companions have just one idea in mind: Snatch some cheeses and make a fast getaway from this enormous disturbing cave. They tell Odysseus, "Let's leave now!" He refuses. He wants to stay and look around; he'd like to know who lives in this place. Odysseus is not only the man who must remember; he is also the man who wants to see, to know, to try out everything the world has to offer, even this subhuman world he's been flung into. Odysseus's curiosity always urges him farther, beyond—which this time could easily be his undoing. In fact that curiosity does cause the death of several companions. A Cyclops soon arrives, with his goats and his sheep and his ram, and the whole throng crowds into the cave.

The Cyclops is enormous, gigantic. He does not immediately notice the little fellows, like fleas, hiding in the niches of the cavern and shaking with fear. Suddenly he does discover them and he addresses Odysseus, who is standing a little ahead of the group: "Who are you?" Odysseus, naturally, starts bluffing. He tells him—first lie—"I've lost my ship," even though his ship lies waiting for him; "my ship is wrecked, so I am totally at your mercy; I've come here with my men to implore your hospitality, we are Greeks, we've fought valiantly for Agamemnon at Troy, we took the city, and now here we are, miserable castaways." The Cyclops responds: "Fine, fine—but you know something? I don't give a damn about all that." He snatches up two of Odysseus's companions by the feet, knocks them against the rock wall, shatters their heads, and swallows them raw. The other sailors are frozen with terror, and Odysseus wonders what he's gotten into. The more so because there is no hope of escape; for the night the Cyclops has closed off the entrance to his lair with a huge boulder that no Greek—not even a sizable team of them—could manage to budge. The next day the scenario is repeated: The Cyclops eats four more men, two in the morning and another two at night. He has devoured six by now—half the crew—and he's utterly delighted. When Odysseus tries cajoling him with honeyed talk, a kind of guest-host bond starts to build between them. Odysseus tells him, "I'm going to give you a gift I believe you'll find very satisfying." A dialogue begins, over the course of which there emerges a personal relationship, a hospitality connection.

The Cyclops introduces himself: Polyphemus. He is a voluble character, and very famous. He asks Odysseus his name. To establish a relationship of host and guest, it is the custom for each party to tell the other who he is, where he comes from, who are his parents, and what is his homeland. Odysseus tells the Cyclops his name is Outis—which means "Nobody": he says, "My friends and relations call me Outis." This is a play on words, for the two syllables of *ou-tis* can be replaced by another term—*me-tis*; *ou* and *me* in Greek are the two prefixes for indicating the negative; but the word *outis* means "nobody," and *metis* means "trickery," "ruse," "cunning." Of course the word *metis* instantly brings to mind Odysseus, who is the very hero of metis—of cunning, of skill at finding a way out of the inextricable; at lying, hoodwinking people, and telling them wild stories; and at getting out of tight spots.

"Outis—Nobody!" exclaims the Cyclops. "Well, since you're Nobody, I'll give you a gift, too—I'll eat you up last!" Whereupon Odysseus hands him his own gift: a cup of the wine Maron had given him, which is sacred nectar. The Cyclops drinks of it, declares it marvelous, pours himself some more. Sated with the cheeses and with the two sailors he's just swallowed, and drunk from the wine, he soon falls asleep.

Now is Odysseus's chance—he heats up an enormous olive-tree trunk he's sharpened to a point. The surviving seamen all help with the carving and then with the maneuver—driving the burning pike into Polyphemus's eye. He wakes up howling. His single eye is blinded. Now he too is consigned to night, to darkness. Naturally he cries out for help, and all his fellow Cyclopes from roundabout come running. Every Cyclops lives by himself, each is master in his own dwelling, the Cyclopes acknowledge no god or master apart from what each is in his home—but still, they do come running. And from outside—since the cavern mouth is blocked—they shout: "Polyphemus! Polyphemus, what's wrong?" "Ah, it's terrible, he's killing me!" "Who's hurt you?" "Nobody! [*outis!*]" "Well, if no one—*metis*—is hurting you, why are you bothering us?" And they leave.

And so Odysseus—who's taken a powder, skipped out, ducked away, vanished behind the name he rigged for himself—is nearly saved. Not entirely, because he still has to get out of the cave with that enormous boulder blocking the door. He sees only one solution: to escape as the sheep are let out to pasture. He will take willow shoots and lash each of the six remaining Greeks beneath the belly of a sheep. He himself will cling to the thick fleece on the underside of Polyphemus's favorite ram. When the giant takes up his position at the doorway of the lair, and has shoved aside the rock blocking it, he passes each animal between his legs and feels along its back to make sure no Greek is riding out on it. He does not notice the Greeks slung hiding underneath. When the ram carrying Odysseus is on its way out, the Cyclops speaks to it—the ram is actually the only being he talks to—and says: "Look at what that dreadful brute Nobody did to me! I'll get even with him for it!" The ram proceeds out of the cavern, and Odysseus exits with it.

The Cyclops rolls the stone back into place, believing that the Greeks are still inside the den, when in fact they are already on their feet outside: They speed down the rocky little trails to the bay where their ship lies camouflaged. They leap aboard, loosen the moorings, and move off from the coast. High above them they can see the Cyclops stuck on the rocky peak beside his cave, blindly hurling huge stones down after them. Odysseus cannot resist the pleasure of taunting and gloating. He shouts, "Cyclops! If anybody asks who blinded your eye, tell them it was Odysseus, son of Laertes—Odysseus of Ithaca, pillager of cities, conqueror of Troy—Odysseus of the thousand tricks!" Well, of course, if you spit up into the air it's likely to fall back in your face: The Cyclops is the son of Poseidon, who is the great god of all the ocean waters—but also god of everything underground: It's Poseidon who sets off earthquakes and tempests. The Cyclops pronounces a solemn curse upon Odysseus—a curse that only works when it uses the target's real name. If Odysseus had taunted Polyphemus again under the name "Nobody," the curse might have failed, but now the Cyclops knows the Greek's true name. He passes it along to his father, Poseidon, and he pleads for revenge: that Odysseus may not return home to the land of Ithaca without suffering a thousand disasters, all his companions dying, his ship capsizing and leaving him alone, lost, a castaway. If Odysseus should somehow nonetheless get through all this alive, the Cyclops wants him to reach Ithaca as a stranger, on a strange ship—not as the long-awaited seafarer making a triumphal return on his own vessel.

Poseidon hears his son's curse. From that episode dates his determination—which will govern all Odysseus's subsequent adventures—that this man shall be forced to the farthest frontier of the shades and of death, and that his ordeals shall be the most dreadful possible. As Odysseus's great protector Athena will explain later, Poseidon could not accept the injury done to his son the Cyclops, and therefore Athena could not intervene; she could only put in an appearance at the very end, when Odysseus's wanderings were over, when he was already nearly home. Why? Because the consequence of tossing Polyphemus's eye out into the

night, of blinding him, is that Odysseus must himself also wander
dark, confusing, and sinister paths.

THE CIRCE IDYLL

The ship sails away from Polyphemus's home and moves on to
Aeolus's island. This is one of the landfalls that some people have
tried to locate exactly, but that by their very nature cannot be
located. Aeolus's island is utterly isolated, and surrounded by a
wall of tall rocks, like a bronze rampart. Aeolus lives here with his
family and in contact with no one else. The Aeolians therefore
reproduce through incest, in a closed matrimonial system. They
exist in total solitude, complete isolation. The island is the hub for
maritime routes, the junction for all the seaways and bearings on
the broad ocean.

Aeolus rules the winds that—depending on where they blow
from—open or close the sea-lanes, and sometimes tangle and confuse them. He welcomes Odysseus with special hospitality and
kindness for being a hero of the Trojan War, one of the men *The
Iliad* will sing. What Odysseus brings him is the news of the world,
the sound of the universe from which he is utterly cut off. He rules
the winds but he has no other power. Odysseus talks, he tells tales,
and Aeolus listens happily. After a few days Aeolus tells him, "I'm
going to give you what you need to leave my island and proceed
with no problem straight for Ithaca." He gives him a goatskin filled
not with wine, like Maron's, but with the sources of all the winds,
the seeds of all the storms. The goatskin is meticulously sealed;
inside it Aeolus has locked the starter, the very germ plasm, of all
the ocean breezes—all but the one wind that blows straight from
his island to Ithaca. He urges Odysseus absolutely not to touch that

goatskin sack. If the other winds should get loose from it, there will be no controlling what might happen. "You see, the only wind blowing in the whole universe right now is the wind that will carry you home to Ithaca." What's left of the crew climbs back aboard, and they set sail directly for Ithaca.

As evening falls, from the deck of his ship Odysseus can make out Ithaca's shores in the distance. He sees with his own eyes the fields of his homeland. Hugely happy, he falls asleep. His lids droop, his eyes close, the way he closed the Cyclops's eye. He is back in the world of the nocturnal, of *hypnos*, of slumber: he is asleep on his ship as it floats toward Ithaca; he neglects to keep watch. Left to themselves, the seamen wonder what Aeolus could have given Odysseus in that goatskin; it must certainly be something very precious. They just want to take a quick look and close it up again. Finally, nearing the shores of Ithaca, they open the sack—and all the other winds escape in tumult, the sea heaves up, the waves crash, the ship tacks sharply and returns along the very path it has just covered. Odysseus, deeply vexed, is back where he started, on Aeolus's island. Aeolus asks what he's doing there. "It's not my fault—I fell asleep, a mistake, I let the darkness of sleep overcome me; I wasn't watching, and my companions opened the sack." This time Aeolus is not welcoming. Odysseus implores him: "Let me try again, give me another chance!" Aeolus is furious, calls him the lowest of the low, a nothing, says he is worthless now, that the gods detest him: "For such a disaster to befall you, you must be accursed! I won't hear another word from you." And so Odysseus and his sailors leave the island without the support they hoped for from Aeolus.

Odysseus's little fleet sails on and reaches a new place, the island of the Laestrygonians. They pull in; there are well-marked harbors and a city. Odysseus is always cannier than the rest; rather than moor his own ship in a kind of natural harbor, he decides to tie up a little farther off, at an inlet some distance away. And because events have made him cautious, rather than go see for himself he sends a squad of his sailors to find out who the inhabitants of the place might be. The sailors clamber up toward the city, and along the way they meet an enormous, hulking girl—a peasantlike, matronly woman, far taller and sturdier than they—who intimidates them. She invites them home with her. "My father is the king; he'll be glad to receive you, and he'll give you whatever you want." The sailors are very pleased, even though they're still uneasy at the size of this charming person. They find her a bit too big and husky. They come before the king of the Laestrygonians, and the minute he sees them, he snatches one of them up and swallows him. Odysseus's men take to their heels and tear back down to the ships, shouting, "Let's get out of here!" Meanwhile, all the other Laestrygonians, stirred up by the king's roar, have rushed out of their houses. They see the Greeks down below frantically busy on the ships, trying to leave the place at top speed. The Laestrygonians fish them out like so many tuna and eat them. All Odysseus's companions perish except those off at a distance on the one ship he had carefully concealed. Odysseus departs with that single ship and its crew.

This one last ship lands next at Aeaea, an island in the Mediterranean. Odysseus and his companions find a spot to hide their ship, then venture forth a ways on land. There are rocks, a forest, vegetation. But like Odysseus, the sailors have grown wary. One of them refuses to move at all. Odysseus urges the others to explore the island. Some twenty sailors set out to reconnoiter, and discover a handsome dwelling, a palace surrounded by flowers, where all seems tranquil. The only thing that bothers them, that seems strange, is that nearby, in the gardens, are a great many wild animals—wolves, lions—who come up to them very good-naturedly, practically rubbing against their legs. The sailors are surprised at this, but they decide they may be in some upside-down universe, an otherworldly place where wild beasts are tame and it is the humans who are deadly. They knock at the door, and a very beautiful young woman opens it. She had been weaving and spinning, and singing in a lovely voice as she worked. She bids them come in, invites them to sit down, offers them a welcoming drink. Into the cup she pours a magic potion, and no sooner have they tasted a drop of the beverage than they turn into swine. They all look like pigs from head to foot—they have pigs' bristles; they grunt and walk and feed like pigs. Circe—this sorceress's name—is delighted at the sight of these pigs, the latest addition to her bestiary. She instantly locks them up in a sty, and proceeds to give them the swill these animals customarily eat.

Odysseus and the rest of his companions are awaiting the return of the sailors gone off to scout the land, and they begin to worry. Now Odysseus ventures into the interior himself to see if he can find any of them. Hermes, that sly and rascally god, appears to him suddenly and tells him what's happened. "She is a sorceress, she has turned your men into swine, she will certainly try to get you to drink the same thing, but you I'll give an antidote so you can fend off the metamorphosis and stay as you are. You will go on being the same Odysseus you always have been—Odysseus himself."

Hermes hands him the sprig of an herb. Odysseus goes back to tell his companions he means to go on into the interior, but they all try to dissuade him: "Don't go. If the others haven't come back to us, they must be dead."

"No," says Odysseus, "I'm going to free them." He swallows Hermes' antidote herb and goes off to see the sorceress.

She invites him in right away; his sword is at his side. She seats him on a fine gilded bench. He makes no mention of his companions, and goes along with the game when she turns to pour the beverage, the potion she hands him to drink. Odysseus drinks down the liquid; she waits and watches, but he does not turn into a pig; it is still Odysseus gazing at her with a friendly smile . . . until he pulls out his sword and lunges at her. She understands, and she says: "You are Odysseus; I knew that with you my spell would not work. What is your desire?"

"First, free my companions," says he.

This confrontation between the sorceress (she is, incidentally, Medea's aunt) and Odysseus—and through him, Hermes the trickster-illusionist god—is the start of a kind of contest and eventually a rapport. Odysseus and Circe will live out a very happy love together. First, though, his comrades must be freed from the spell. Why did Circe turn them into pigs? She does the same to every traveler who arrives on her island. Why? Because she is alone, and she wants to surround herself with living creatures who cannot leave. The story states quite directly that in turning them all into pigs or other animals, what she's hoping for is that they will forget the return home, forget their past—forget they are men. And indeed that did happen to Odysseus's men, though they do nonetheless retain some clarity of mind: They still have a kind of intelligence, such that when they see him, they are very glad—they recognize him. Circe touches them with her wand. They instantly turn back to human form, and after the ordeal they are far handsomer, younger, better-looking than they had been before. Going through this condition of pigdom has been a kind of initiation, as if enacting the progression toward death were necessary for coming through such an experience more youthful and beautiful and alive. That is what happens to them as they turn back into men. Circe might have slaughtered them; then they would have lost *nous*, or intellect: Dead people, for instance, are entirely wrapped in darkness; they no longer have *nous*—except for one, Tiresias, who will appear again later. But what Odysseus's shipmates lived through was not exactly death; it was a bestialization that cut them off from the human world, that caused them to forget their past but that endowed them with a fresh new glow of youth as they emerged.

Thereafter Odysseus and Circe live a veritable idyll. They may even have had children, say some accounts, but that is far from certain. They simply love each other; they make love. Circe sings in her beautiful voice and, of course, Odysseus gathers in the shipmates who had hung back; they are highly mistrustful at first, but he hasn't much trouble convincing them: "Come, come, you're in no danger now." They dwell on the island a long time. Circe, that magician, was wrong to make pigs or wild beasts of every man who turned up on her domain, but she is no ogre or wicked witch. When they are settled in with her, she goes to great lengths to make them happy.

Still, Odysseus's companions—who obviously don't enjoy the sojourn quite as much as their master does, since they do not have access to Circe's bed—start to weary of the place. When they remind Odysseus that he should think about the journey home, Circe does not protest or try to hold him back. She says, "If you want to leave, of course you should leave," and she provides him with all the information she can to make their voyage a good one. In particular she tells him, "Listen: The next lap of your journey should take you to the country of the Cimmerians, where day never comes, the land of night, the land of constant fog, the mouth to Hades." This time it is more than a matter of being flung to the outermost bounds of the human, at risk of forgetting one's past and one's humanity; here he will touch the very frontier of the world of the dead. Circe instructs Odysseus how to proceed: "Land at thus-and-such a place; go ashore on foot; you'll see a trench; carry flour with you; take a ram and slit its throat, sprinkle its blood on the ground, and the crowd of the *eidola* will spring up— doubles, phantoms, souls of the dead. Look for Tiresias's ghost and seize it; give him blood from your ram to drink, and he'll come back to a degree of life and tell you what to do next."

THE NAMELESS, THE FACELESS

Odysseus and his companions do set off, and they reach the land of the dead. Odysseus carries out the required rituals: He stands at the trench, he has poured out the flour and slaughtered the ram, the blood is ready to be drunk. And he does see coming toward him the crowd of those who are nobody, *outis*, as he once pretended to be—the nameless, the *nonumnoi*, people who no longer have faces, who are no longer visible, who have no more substance. They form a vague mass of beings who used to be individual persons but can no longer be distinguished. From that mass swarming past him there rises a terrifying, undifferentiated sound. They have no name, they do not speak; it is chaotic noise. Odysseus is seized with terror at the spectacle, which to his eyes and ears seems the threat of utter dissolution into formless magma, with his own skillful speech drowned in inarticulate noise and his glory, his fame, his renown obliterated, in danger of disappearing in that dark night.

Meanwhile Tiresias appears. Odysseus gives him the ram's blood to drink, and the seer tells him that he will indeed reach home, where Penelope awaits him, and gives him much other news. Agamemnon is dead, and Odysseus also sees the shades of several heroes; he sees his mother; he finds Achilles and questions him. Having himself drunk a little of the restorative blood, Achilles speaks. What does he say, now when everyone is singing his praises, when his *kleos*—his fame—glitters so brightly throughout the wide world, when he is the very model of the hero and people say that even in the underworld his glory is acknowl-edged? Listen to him: "I would rather be the lowest mud-caked miserable peasant in the dungheap, the poorest pauper, but living in sunlight, than be Achilles down here in the world of shadows that is Hades." What Achilles says in *The Odyssey* is the opposite of what *The Iliad* proclaimed: that Achilles had the choice between a short, glorious life and a long life without glory, and he had never hesitated or doubted for a moment: He would choose a glorious life and heroic death in the flower of youth, because the glory of a short life ending in a fine death was worth far more than anything else. Now he says exactly the opposite: Once a man dies, given the choice he would rather be a poor louse-ridden peasant alive in the most benighted backwater of Greece than great Achilles in the world of the dead.

Odysseus hears this confession and sets sail again. He stops back at Circe's island, and she welcomes him once more, feeds him and his shipmates, provides them bread and wine for the voyage, and then sets their course. She particularly tells them how to deal with the dreadful danger of the Wandering Rocks, the Planctes—great loose crags that clash together just as a ship sails between them. To avoid them ships must navigate between Scylla and Charybdis—Charybdis is a whirlpool chasm that can suck them under, and Scylla a rock as tall as the sky, the lair of a monster that snatches up passersby and devours them. Circe warns that they will encounter not only the giant rocks and the dreadful choice between the two perils Scylla and Charybdis; they will also come upon the Sirens on their little isle. Any ship that sails near and hears the Sirens sing is lost, for seafarers cannot resist the bewitch-ment of that song, and their ship runs aground on the reef and shatters.

Odysseus's vessel does come within sight of the singers' rock. What does the ingenious captain do? He has got himself some beeswax, and just as they see the little island with the perching Sirens—they are bird-women, or women-birds, singers with glorious voices—he plugs the crewmen's ears with the wax, so that they hear nothing. But he himself will not forgo hearing them. He is not only the man of loyalty and of memory, but, as in the Cyclops episode, he is also the man who wants to know things, including things that he ought not to. He would never sail near the Sirens and not hear their song, not learn what they sing and how they sing it. Therefore he leaves his own ears unstopped, but he has his crew lash him firmly to the mast so that he cannot move. The ship sails on, and just as it draws near to the isle of the Sirens, suddenly there is what the Greeks call *galēnē*—an utter calm; the wind drops, there is not a sound, the vessel falls almost motionless, and in that calm the Sirens sound their song. What do they sing? They address Odysseus as if they were Muses, as if they were the daughters of memory—those figures inspiring Homer as he sings his poems, inspiring the bard as he tells the grand exploits of the heroes. They say: "Odysseus, Odysseus, glorious Odysseus beloved—come, come, hear us, we will tell you all, we will sing the glory of the heroes, and sing your own glory too."

But meanwhile, even as these beauties are revealing the Truth with a capital T—that is, the precise story of all that has happened—meanwhile their island is ringed by a mass of corpses, flesh decomposing in the hot sun on the beach. These are the bodies of all the men who succumbed to the Sirens' call and died. The Sirens are both the appeal of the yearning for knowledge, erotic attraction—they are the essence of seduction—and death. What they say to Odysseus is in a sense what will be said of him when he no longer exists, when he will have crossed the frontier between the world of light and that of shadows, when he will have become the Odysseus of the story men have made about him, and whose adventures I am recalling at this very moment. They are reciting them to him while he is still alive, as if he were already dead; or rather as if he were in some place and time where the frontier between living and dead, between light of life and darkness of death, were not firmly fixed but were still unstable, porous—crossable. They are drawing him toward the death that will consecrate his glory—the death Achilles said he would not choose again, even though when he was still alive he had wanted that glory, because only death can bring humans an undying renown.

Odysseus hears the Sirens' song as the vessel moves slowly by; he struggles to get to the singers, but his sailors bind his ropes tighter. Finally the ship pulls past the Sirens forever and comes to the great rocks ramming and crashing together. Odysseus risks Scylla over Charybdis, and the result is that when the ship moves between them, some of his crewmen are snatched up by Scylla, with her six heads and twelve-clawed dogs' paws, and swallowed down alive. Only a few get through; there are not many left. In a while they reach Thrinacia, the island of the sun god. The place does belong to the sun, that all-seeing eye. There are cattle there that are divine, immortal; they do not reproduce. They are a set number, as many as the days of the year, and this must never be changed, to either more or fewer. They are all splendid animals, and one of Tiresias's revelations to Odysseus had been this: "When you reach the island of the sun, under no circumstances must you touch one animal of that sacred herd. If you do not lay a finger on them, then you have some chance of getting home. If you do touch them, all is lost." Naturally, before landing on Thrinacia, Odysseus recalls that command, and he warns his crew: "We are coming to where the sun god's cattle are grazing, but it is forbidden to lay a hand on them. The animals are untouchable; they are sacred. The sun keeps a very jealous eye on them. We will eat our own provisions here on the ship; we will not be stopping on that island."

But his sailors are exhausted. They have just come through enormous perils; some of their comrades lost their lives there; they are done in, exhausted, and they tell Odysseus: "You must be made of iron to refuse to land there!"

Eurylochus, the first mate, speaks for the whole crew; he says, "We're stopping." "Fine," says Odysseus, "but we will eat only the provisions Circe gave us." The sorceress herself drank nectar and ambrosia, but she had given them bread and wine, human foods. The ship lands, they disembark onto the strand, and they eat their own provisions. The next day a gale rises; it blows for days and days so that they cannot leave. They are caught on the island, and gradually their reserves, their food supplies, give out. Hunger grips them, wracks their stomachs.

Hunger is one of those entities the poet Hesiod lists among the children of Night. She gave birth to Limos—Hunger—along with Crime, Darkness, Forgetting, Sleep. Forgetting and Sleep and Hunger: This baleful trio of somber, dark powers lies in wait.

In this case hunger sets in first; the sailors resort to fishing. They catch something now and then, but not enough; there is almost nothing to eat. Odysseus once again leaves his companions, climbs to the high ground to see what the island may offer, and falls asleep. Again our Odysseus is caught up in the dark mantle of sleep sent by the gods. While he slumbers hunger has free rein, and through Eurylochus it speaks to all the men: "We're not going to simply stand here and die of starvation! Look at those splendid beasts—the very sight of them makes my mouth water." Taking advantage of Odysseus's absence, of his being closed away in his slumbering world and not right there watching out, they surround the herd. They drive down and sacrifice several animals; they chase and corner them, slash their throats, and put them up to cook. They drop some chunks into cauldrons, broil others over the fire. Just then Odysseus awakes on his hill. He smells the aroma of grilled fat and meat. Suddenly struck with dreadful anguish, he cries out to the gods: "Gods, you have tricked me! You sent me the darkness of this sleep—not a restful sleep, but a sleep of forgetting and death! And now I wake to find this crime!" He goes down, rails at his comrades, but they—disregarding their orders and their promise—their only concern is eating.

Yet certain uncanny things occur: Those beasts, who've been sliced into pieces and cooked, continue to low as if they were alive. They have died but are still alive because they are immortal. The sacrifice was carried out but in corrupt and faulty fashion, as if it were a hunt for wild animals; this mixed the savage and the civilized together. More strange things occur, but Odysseus's companions go right on eating, stuffing their bellies, and then they drop off to sleep. Instantly the waves grow calm, the wind falls. Time to embark again. They gather on board, and no sooner has the ship left the island than Helios, the sun god speaks—not to Poseidon this time but to Zeus: "Look what they've done to me! They've slaughtered my cattle! You must avenge me. If you do not, I will cease to shine for the immortal gods in the empyrean, and I will cease to shine for mortal humans who depend on day following night on earth; I shall go shine for those down below—for the dead! I will go down into Hades and turn my light on the shadows! And the rest of you—you will all live in darkness, gods and men alike!"

Zeus talks him out of it. "I'll take care of this whole thing," he declares.

Through a lapse in vigilance, Odysseus had allowed his sailors to commit the sin of mixing sacred and profane, the sacrifice and the hunt—muddling everything together and bringing on the risk that the sun might light up the night, and where the sun ought to shine it would be night instead. They cast off the lines again, but they have sailed scarcely a few yards when, from on high, Zeus sends shadows over the sky. The ship is suddenly gripped by darkness, the waves heave up, thunder blasts over the ship, the mast cracks and topples, crushing the skull of the pilot, who tumbles into the sea. Wrenched and tossed, the vessel shatters into a thousand pieces. All Odysseus's shipmates seem turned into animals, bobbing like crows atop the waves. Odysseus drifts for nine days, clinging to a spar. Finally the waves cast him ashore, utterly exhausted, on Calypso's island.

CALYPSO'S ISLAND

Odysseus's ship is blasted and shattered, and all his remaining sailors have drowned, their bodies bobbing like crows on the waves. Odysseus alone has come through. He clings to a mast, a spar from the ship, and suddenly the current is rushing him backward, toward Charybdis and a drastic situation. He escapes again by a near miracle. For another nine days, alone, exhausted, he floats in the seas with the currents carrying him this way and that at their will, to the far edge of the world. And then, like any shipwrecked seaman on the verge of letting himself drown, he touches down on Calypso's island. It is a place at the end of the world, past even the bounds of the sea; vast stretches of water separate it from gods and men both. It is *nowhere*. Odysseus sprawls exhausted, and Calypso gathers him up. Unlike what happened in Circe's country, where Odysseus and his sailors themselves came to the nymph to implore her compassion, here it is Calypso who moves to save Odysseus.

He stays there for an eternity—five years, ten, fifteen, no matter, for time has stopped. He is outside space, outside time. One day is like another. He is living an erotic intimacy with Calypso, a

constant infatuated closeness, with no other contact, no other people, in utter solitude together. When nothing happens, nothing
changes, and there is no event to mark them, all days are alike.
Odysseus is outside the world, outside time, here in Calypso's
home. Toward him she is love itself, full of solicitude. But she is
also what her name suggests (it comes from the Greek verb
kaluptein, "to hide"): a person hidden away somewhere—and
hiding Odysseus from all eyes.

A MINIATURE PARADISE

Indeed, that is how Homer begins his account of Odysseus's
adventure. For ten years the hero is hidden away in Calypso's
domain. He lives with her; he has reached the end of the journey,
the end of his odyssey. And then suddenly the plot thickens. And
Athena steps in too, taking advantage of a moment when the god
Poseidon is off guard—Poseidon, who has been pursuing
Odysseus with his bitterness, his hatred over his blinded son
Cyclops. Poseidon is off visiting the distant tribe of the Ethiops, as
he often does—to feast with those mythical figures. Legend
describes them as a race forever young and fragrant with the scent
of violets—who have no experience of decay and who need not
even toil, because every morning, out on the great prairies, they
find what animal and vegetable sustenance they need, all prepared
and cooked as in the golden age. The Ethiops live at the two
extremes of the world, the farthest east and the farthest west.
Poseidon visits them there; he eats and plays and takes his pleasure with them.

   So Athena takes the occasion to tell her father, Zeus, that
things cannot go on this way—that all the Greek heroes who did

not die on Trojan soil or perish at sea on the return voyage are now back at home, have rejoined their families, their homes, and their wives, and only Odysseus—the pious Odysseus, her protégé—is still shut away with that Calypso. Faced with his daughter Athena's determination, and in Poseidon's absence, Zeus makes his decision. He throws the dice and reads the omens: Odysseus is to come home. Easily said, but it will still take Calypso's letting him go. Hermes is assigned to see to it. He is very unhappy with the mission: He has never set foot on Calypso's island, and one can see why, since it is a kind of nowhere place. She is far from the gods, far from men. Getting to her requires crossing an enormous stretch of salty sea.

Hermes dons his winged sandals, and now he is swift as lightning, swift as thought. Grumbling that he's only doing the errand under orders and against his will, he alights on Calypso's isle. He is astonished to discover this nowhere place—the little island is like a miniature paradise. There are gardens, forests, fountains, springs, flowers, and prettily arranged caverns where Calypso sings and spins and weaves and makes love with Odysseus. Hermes is dazzled. He approaches Calypso. They have not met before, but they recognize each other. "Well now, my dear Hermes—what brings you here? I don't see much of you." "You're right," Hermes answers. "If it were up to me, I would never have come, but I have an order from Zeus. He's made up his mind: You must let Odysseus leave. Zeus feels there's no good reason why Odysseus should be the only one, of all the heroes of the Trojan War, not to have gotten home." Calypso retorts, "Please don't talk nonsense. I know why you want me to give up Odysseus. It's because you gods are miserable folks, worse than humans; you're all jealous. You can't bear the idea that a goddess should cohabit with a mortal. The idea that for years I've been living here peacefully with this man in my bed—

it drives you mad." Having no choice in the matter, she adds, "But fine, all right—I'll send him back."

Hermes returns to Olympus. From then on the story itself ranges back and forth. Odysseus's travels thus far had drawn him away from the world of men, and taken him to the land of the dead among the Cimmerians, to the outermost edge of the world of light, the world of the living. Now here he is out of action in this kind of uncanny parenthesis, isolated on the wide ocean. His wanderings had stopped short nearly ten years back, in the solitary love duet with Calypso.

Where was Odysseus when Hermes stepped into Calypso's cave? He had gone off alone onto a headland; looking out over the sea as it heaved hugely before him, he was crying every last tear in his body. He was virtually turned to liquid. Every bit of moist vitality he had within him was pouring out through his eyes, his skin—he could no longer bear it. Why? Because he was missing his past life, missing Ithaca and his wife, Penelope. Calypso could not help but know that Odysseus still thought about his journey home—that he was the "homecoming man." But she harbored the hope that she might somehow make him forget the homecoming, find a way to keep him from recalling what he used to be. How would she do it? Odysseus had visited the land of the dead; there among the specters he had heard Achilles say how dreadful it is to be dead, how this phantom with no life or consciousness that a person becomes—this nameless shade—is the very worst future a man can imagine. And now, after his long journey and all his ordeals, Calypso offers him the chance to be immortal and to stay forever young, no longer to fear death and old age.

In formulating that double promise, she knew what she was doing. There is in fact a story she could not have missed; everyone knew it: Eos—Dawn—fell in love with a very beautiful young man called Tithonus. She carried him off to live with her and, claiming she could not do without the boy, asked Zeus to grant him immortality so she might never be separated from him. With an ironic little smile, Zeus told her, "Fine on the immortality." And so Tithonus arrives at Eos's palace on Olympus as a young man, with the privilege of living forever. But after some time he was worse than an old man, because at 150 or 200 years old, he has become a kind of insect, utterly shriveled, unable to speak or move, feeding on nothing. A living ghost.

IMPOSSIBLE FORGETTING

That is not what Calypso is offering Odysseus; she is proposing that he become an actual god; that is to say, an eternally youthful immortal. In hopes of making Odysseus's shipmates forget their journey home, Circe had turned them into beasts, lower than human. Calypso has the same goal—to bring Odysseus to forget Ithaca and Penelope—but her proposal is that Odysseus metamorphose not into an animal but into a god. The drama, the problematic knot of the story, is that Odysseus confronts this dilemma: He has seen what death is, he saw it when he visited the land of the Cimmerians at the mouth of Hades; he saw it again with the Sirens, who were singing his glory from their islet rimmed with corpses. Here Calypso is offering him nondeath and eternal youth, but there is a price to pay for achieving that metamorphosis. The price is that he remain with her, that he forget his homeland. And furthermore, if he stays on with Calypso, he will remain in concealment and thus cease to be himself—Odysseus, the homecoming hero.

Odysseus is the man of remembrance, willing to undergo any ordeal, any hardship, for the sake of fulfilling his destiny, which is being flung out to the very frontiers of the human and yet managing—knowing how, and determining—to come back and to take up his own self again. And becoming an immortal would mean renouncing all that. From the standpoint of a Greek, what Odysseus is being offered is not his own immortality but an anonymous one. When Athena disguises herself as Mentor—a wise old man who is a friend of Odysseus—and appears in Ithaca to visit Odysseus's son, Telemachus, she tells him, "You know, your father is a very shrewd man, very wily; I'm sure he's going to come back, so be ready—you're going to have to help him. Go ask around in the other cities of Greece, see if anyone has news of him. Don't just sit there inert, mourning—take action!"

Telemachus tells her that he is not certain the man is actually his father: Penelope, his mother, has told him his father is Odysseus, but he has never seen him. Indeed, Odysseus left when Telemachus had just been born; he was only a few months old. Now Telemachus is twenty, and Odysseus sailed away twenty years ago. His father is a foreigner, the boy tells Athena—and not only to him; the gods have made him a person who is utterly unseen and unheard, invisible and inaudible. He has disappeared as if the monstrous Harpies had snatched him away and he was erased from the world of men. No one knows what's become of him. Adds Telemachus, "If at least he died fighting on Greek soil, or on the way home with his ships, his companions would have brought him back to us, and we would have put up a burial mound and a *sema*, a tombstone with his name carved on it. Then he would have always been somehow with us. And in any case, he would have bequeathed us—bequeathed me, his son, and his whole family—a deathless glory, *kleos aphthiton*. Whereas now he has vanished from the world; he is erased, swallowed up, *akleos*—without glory."

What Calypso is offering Odysseus, then, is immortal life, eternal youth, but in a cloud of obscurity, with no one hearing talk of him, no human pronouncing his name, and of course with no bard singing his praises. As Pindar says in one of his poems, when a great feat has been accomplished it should not remain "hidden." (His word, *kaluptein*, is the same that underlies Calypso's name.) If that exploit is to live on, it requires the poetic praise song of a great bard.

Of course, if Odysseus stays on in Calypso land, there is no more *Odyssey*, and therefore no more Odysseus. Thus the dilemma remains as follows: either an immortality that is anonymous, nameless—which means that, even living forever, Odysseus will be like the dead folk of Hades, who are called the "nameless" because they have lost their identity; or, should he choose the opposite, then an existence that is mortal—that ends in death, yes, but one in which he will keep that self, memorable and crowned with glory.

Odysseus tells Calypso his choice is to go home.

He no longer feels desire, no *himeros* or *eros*, for that curly-haired nymph with whom he has lived in intimacy for ten years. He may sleep with her that night, but because she wants it. As for himself, he no longer cares to. His sole desire is to take back his mortal life . . . and he even desires to die. His *himeros*—longing— is focused on mortal life, he yearns to complete his life.

Calypso asks, "Are you so very much attached to Penelope, do you choose her over me? You think her more beautiful?"

"No, no, look, of course not," Odysseus answers. "You're a goddess—you're more beautiful, you are taller, you are more marvelous than Penelope, I know that. But Penelope is Penelope— she's my life, my wife, my country."

"Fine," says Calypso. "I understand."

So she gives the necessary orders, and she helps him to build a raft. Together they cut down trees and trim them to shape a good solid raft with a mast. Thus does Odysseus leave Calypso, and a new adventure series begins.

NAKED AND INVISIBLE

He sets forth on the raft. All goes well. After several days' sailing, Odysseus sees what looks like a shield on the sea: the island of Phaeacia. Poseidon, who has finished his holiday in Ethiop and is on his way back to Olympus, looks down from high in the sky and sees a raft with some fellow clinging to the mast; he recognizes Odysseus. He goes into a rage. He hadn't heard a word about this nut for ten years now, but he understands instantly that the other gods have decided otherwise, and that Zeus has made a choice. He cannot resist: Again he sends a thunderbolt against the raft, it shatters, and Odysseus is swimming among the tossing waves, gulping water and preparing to die. Then, fortunately, another deity spots him—Ino/Leucothea, the white goddess, who sometimes appears to the shipwrecked in great storms and rescues them. She goes to Odysseus and hands him a veil, a sash, and says, "Put this on and you will not perish. But throw it off before you set foot on land." Odysseus takes the sash, swims with difficulty, approaches the shore—but each time he tries to touch down the undertow pulls him away again. Eventually, farther along the cliffs he makes out a kind of little cove, the mouth of a creek or river where the outflow keeps the waves from crashing against the rocks. He swims over there; night is falling, he can't go on, he is worn out. He throws off the talisman sash, tentatively makes his way ashore, and collapses a little farther up the slope. He hides beneath a leafy thicket, wondering who lives there—what new danger threatens him. Despite his exhaustion he is determined not to shut his eyes. For many nights he has not slept, he is grimy with brine from floating in the sea for days and days with no chance to cleanse himself. He is caked in salt, his hair is filthy and his whiskers shaggy. He stretches out, and immediately Athena, who has not stepped in for a long time, returns and puts him to sleep.

This island is the home of the Phaeacians, halfway between the world of men—of Ithaca, of Greece—and an extraordinary, miraculous world where cannibals live side by side with goddesses. In fact the Phaeacians' profession is transport. They are seamen with magical boats—boats that travel under their own power, at high speed and in any chosen direction, with no need to steer them or to propel them by oars. The inhabitants are a little like Hermes, the god of journeys and crossings, of traffic between one world and the other. This island, furthermore, is not in direct contact with the outside. The Phaeacians are ferrymen, but no one ever comes to their land, no human foreigner ever ventures there. Some gods, on the other hand, do occasionally stop by in person, and they appear in their true nature, with no need for disguise.

Odysseus is still hidden in his thicket asleep when dawn breaks. In the royal palace, the king has a daughter fifteen or sixteen years old—Nausicaa. She is of marrying age, but it is probably no easy thing to find a man here in Phaeacia who might answer to her father's expectations of a son-in-law. She had a dream the night before—it was doubtless Athena who gave it a certain turn: She dreamed of a possible husband. In the morning she calls together her maidservants, who come running and gather up the household laundry; they will wash it in the clear waters of a stream and then lay out the fine fabrics, the sheets and clothing, to dry on the riverbank rocks. They bring a mule cart to carry all the soiled linen to the stream. With the washing done, the girls set about playing ball. One clumsy maidservant misses the ball Nausicaa tosses her, and it falls into the stream. The girls cry out sharply. Odysseus wakes with a start.

He emerges from his shrubbery and observes the scene. He is as naked as a worm, terrifying to see—and because he is wary, his glance glitters with menace. At the sight of him the girls scatter like frightened birds. All but one—Nausicaa, the tallest, the loveliest, and whose position among these girls is like the goddess Artemis's amid her followers—ever a notch higher. Nausicaa does not flinch. She stands unmoving. Odysseus sees her. She gazes back, probably wondering who this dreadful fellow might be, this monster, but she does not move: She is the king's daughter. Thereupon Odysseus, dreadful to behold but sweet to hear—he is the man of skillful talk—asks her, "Who are you? Are you a goddess with her followers? I am a castaway, tossed here by misfortune. You know, when I look at you I think of a young palm tree I saw at Delos once, on a voyage—a slender young palm stretching straight up to the height of the sky. I was struck with wonder at the sight of it; I stood there ecstatic—and now the same with you, maiden. Looking at you, seeing you, I am struck with wonder."

She answers: "Your words belie your appearance; you do not seem to be an evil man, a *kakos*." She calls her maidens and asks them to see to this man. "Give him what he needs to bathe and dress."

Odysseus steps into the stream, washes away all the brine, the sea scum smearing his skin; he bathes and slips into the clothing. That done, Athena of course endows him with grace and beauty. She makes him handsomer, younger, stronger, and she anoints him with *charis*—grace, radiance, charm. . . . Odysseus gleams with beauty and appeal. Nausicaa looks at him, and privately to her servants she says, "You know, earlier this man looked unseemly, *aeikelios*—dreadful—and now he is seemly, *eikelos*, like the gods in heaven."

At that moment the idea germinates in Nausicaa's head that this foreigner sent by the gods is somehow available, that before her stands the possibility of the spouse, the husband she had dreamed of. When Odysseus asks her what he should do next, she urges him to go to the palace of her father, Alcinous, and her mother, Arete. "Take care as you go there; I'll return to the palace myself—I'll load the mules with the wash and go on ahead with my women—but you know, it's best if we're not seen together. First of all because a foreigner is unusual here, everyone knows everyone, if they see someone unfamiliar, people will certainly wonder; and if on top of that they see him in my company, you can imagine what they might think. So you set out after I do: Follow the road, and when you get to thus-and-such a place, go into the beautiful palace—it's got marvelous gardens, with flowers and fruits at every season. There is a harbor as well, with fine ships. Go into the great hall, and lie at the feet of my mother, Arete; embrace her knees and ask for her hospitality. Until you reach the palace, though, do not stop along the way, and speak to no one."

Nausicaa leaves, and Odysseus notices a little girl nearby. It is Athena, in disguise. She tells him, "Follow the directions of the king's daughter, but even so, I'm going to make you invisible besides, so that you won't run into problems on the way. Even while you're invisible, you must not look at anyone else. Meet nobody's eye; to be invisible one must not look at other people either."

Odysseus obeys all her advice and enters the palace to prostrate himself before the queen. He is still invisible as he crosses the hall where all the Phaeacian nobility are assembled. He approaches the throne where King Alcinous and Queen Arete are seated. Only then does Athena disperse the cloud, and in stupefaction the Phaeacians see this foreigner clasping their queen's knees. Arete and Alcinous decide to welcome him as their guest. They hold a great festival, and in its course Odysseus displays matchless athletic abilities. One of the king's sons does his best to provoke him, but Odysseus keeps his composure. He throws the discus farther than the prince, and thus proves himself a man of valor, a hero. A bard is called to sing. Odysseus is seated beside the king, and the bard begins to tell of the Trojan War. He recounts the great exploits and the death of some of Odysseus's companions. At that Odysseus can no longer contain himself. He lowers his head and pulls his garment over his eyes to hide his tears, but Alcinous sees through his ploy; he understands that to be so overcome by the song, this man beside him must be one of the heroes the bard is celebrating. He stops the song and, then, in a way, Odysseus takes it up: He confesses his identity—"I am Odysseus"—and goes on to recount, like a bard, a large part of his adventures.

The king decides to take Odysseus back to his home in Ithaca. He does so because he must, but not without regret, for he too had his daughter in mind. He gives Odysseus to understand that, if he should choose to stay here with the Phaeaceans, and sleep with Nausicaa, he would make an ideal son-in-law. He would carry on the royal line. Odysseus explains that his world, his life, is in Ithaca, and asks that the king help him get back to them. Toward evening the Phaeacians gather gifts for him and fill one of their own ships with them, and Odysseus climbs aboard. He says his farewells to all—to the king, the queen, Nausicaa—just as he had said good-bye to Calypso and to Circe. The ship floats off and moves toward human waters. This ship transports Odysseus from the world of nowhere—the place he has lived in at the frontiers of the human race, on the margins of light and of life—back toward his fatherland, his home, in Ithaca.

A DUBIOUS BEGGAR

Scarcely is he aboard than he falls asleep, and the ship sails on of its own accord. The Phaeacian seamen arrive in Ithaca on a beach with a spreading olive tree, the mouth of a nymphs' cave, and mountain peaks. It is a kind of natural harbor, with two great facing walls of rock. The Phaeacians lay the sleeping Odysseus on the shore, beneath that olive tree, and leave as they came. But Poseidon, from on high, has seen how things are going. He has been foiled once again: Odysseus is home. The god decides to avenge himself on the Phaeacians. Just as their ship reaches port, he gives a great blow with his trident, the ship turns to stone, and, taking root in the sea, becomes a rocky isle. The Phaeacians can no longer act as ferrymen between the worlds. The door through which Odysseus passed at the start of the story, and again on his way home—that door is shut forever. The human world is now one integral thing, and Odysseus is part of it for good.

The next morning at dawn, he awakes and looks about at this landscape so familiar to him, where he spent his whole youth, and he recognizes nothing. In fact Athena has decided that before he gets home our hero must undergo a complete transformation. Why? Because during his absence, and particularly during the last ten years of it, a hundred suitors, believing Odysseus dead or at least gone forever, have occupied his palace. They met there, spent all their time there; they ate and they drank, depleting his flocks, emptying his storerooms of wine and grain, as they waited for Penelope to choose someone among them, which she has been unwilling to do. She has tried a thousand stratagems: She has insisted that she cannot marry until she is sure her husband is dead; then she claims she cannot marry before weaving her father-in-law, Laertes, a burial shroud. Now she is in the women's quarters, while in the great hall where they feast, the suitors bed down after the banquets with those among the servant girls who are willing to betray their masters' cause. The suitors commit a thousand other follies there as well.

In her chamber Penelope weaves at her cloth the whole day

long, but each evening she undoes all the day's labor. Thus for almost two years she has managed to put off the suitors on grounds that the work is not finished. But one of the servants eventually reveals the truth to the suitors, and they demand that Penelope make a decision.

What Athena wants, of course, is to keep Odysseus from making Agamemnon's mistake—coming back in his own identity and falling into the trap set by those who await him. He must therefore reappear in a disguise, incognito. To do this, to make sure that no one recognizes him, it is also necessary that he himself not recognize the familiar landscape of his homeland. When Athena appeared before Odysseus on the shore where he was set down, she explained the situation: "There are suitors there; you must kill them. You will have to get the support of your son, Telemachus, now that he's back from abroad, and of Eumaeus, the swineherd, and of Philoetius, the cowherd; that way you may manage to beat them. I'll help you, but I must first transform you completely." He accepts her proposal, and she has him view Ithaca in its true light, as it actually is. The cloud dissipates, and he recognizes his homeland.

Just as she had earlier given him grace and beauty for his encounter with Nausicaa, Athena now clothes him in old age and ugliness. His hair falls out, he goes bald, his skin withers, his eyes grow rheumy, he is stooped and ragged, he reeks; everything about him has the hideous look of a misshapen beggar. His plan, in fact, is to go into his palace, to play the lowest of the low, a pauper begging for food, to submit to every insult in order to assess the situation, find accomplices, and lay his hands on his bow. He used to be the only one who could string that bow; now he means to try unobtrusively to get hold of it quickly and use it to kill the suitors.

He arrives at the palace gates and comes across old Eumaeus, his swineherd. He asks the old man who he is, and who lives in the palace. Eumaeus answers, "My master, Odysseus, went away twenty years ago, no one knows what happened to him; it's a terrible misfortune, everything is falling apart: My lady's suitors are within, the household is ruined, they are plundering the foodstores, the flocks; they order me to bring in suckling pigs every day for them to eat, it's horrible!"

The two of them are walking toward the palace entryway, and there at the gate—upon a dungheap, the pile of household filth set out every morning—Odysseus sees a dog, Argus. He is twenty years older, he is like Odysseus, his double as a dog—that is to say, repugnant, fleabitten, feeble, barely able to move. Odysseus asks Eumeus, "That dog—what was he like when he was young?" "Oh, he was amazing. He was a hunter, he'd go after hares and never miss a one, he'd bring them on back. . . ." "I see," says Odysseus, still moving forward. Old Argus lifts his muzzle slightly and recognizes his master, but he hasn't even the strength to get up. He just twitches his tail and points his ears.

Odysseus sees the old dog, decrepit as he is, recognizing him, the way dogs recognize: by some instant scent. For humans to recognize Odysseus after so many years, so many changes, they will need *semata*, signs and markers that serve as proofs; they will ponder these signs to reconstruct Odysseus's identity. But not the dog: From the very first moment he knows this is Odysseus; he scents him. At the sight of his old dog, Odysseus is utterly overcome; near tears, he moves away quickly. The dog dies. Eumaeus hasn't noticed a thing. They walk on. At the entrance to the palace they meet another beggar, Irus, a younger man than Odysseus appears to be. Irus is the established beggar at the house; he has been there a long time, he picks up an occasional tip, a frequent slap, as the suitors feast and play. Straight out he says to Odysseus in his guise as beggar like himself: "Just what do you think you're doing here? Get out; this is my territory, don't hang around here, you won't get a thing." Odysseus answers, "We'll see about that." They enter together. The suitors are at table in the midst of a meal; the servants are bringing them food and drink. They laugh at seeing two beggars instead of one. Irus begins to pick a quarrel with Odysseus; this amuses the suitors, who joke about it and lay bets that Irus, as the younger man, will beat the old fellow handily. At first Odysseus refuses to fight; then he agrees to settle the quarrel by boxing. Everyone gathers round to watch. Odysseus tucks up his tunic a bit, and the suitors see that the thighs of this flaccid old codger are still firm, and that the outcome of the match is not so predictable after all. The fight begins, and effortlessly, in less time than it takes to tell it, Odysseus knocks Irus unconscious, amid delighted shouts and bravos from all the assembly. Odysseus tosses Irus out of the palace, but then he is subjected to a barrage of insults and humiliations himself, and one of the suitors won't settle for words alone. Across the table, at full force, he flings a cow's foot aimed to wound Odysseus; he hits him on the shoulder and does hurt him. Telemachus steps in to calm things down, declaring, "This man is my guest—I will not have him insulted or ill treated."

ODYSSEUS'S SIGNATURE SCAR

Odysseus makes himself known to a certain number of people whose support he wants. First to Telemachus, back from his expedition to seek news of his father. On his way home he successfully avoided an ambush set for him by the suitors, alerted to his departure: These fellows hoped to use the occasion to kill him and marry Penelope unopposed. Marrying Penelope means taking over Odysseus's bed—the royal couch—and thus becoming ruler of Ithaca. Alerted by Athena, Telemachus avoids the trap: He disembarks at an unexpected location and heads directly for old Eumaeus's dwelling.

The first encounter between Telemachus and Odysseus: Eumaeus leaves to notify Penelope that her son is still alive. Odysseus and Telemachus are alone in the swineherd's tiny hut when Athena appears. Odysseus can see her, and the dogs scent her presence—they are terrified, the hairs stand up along their spines, they lower their tails, they hide beneath the table. Telemachus, though, sees nothing. The goddess signals Odysseus to join her outside. There she touches him with her magic wand, and Odysseus returns to his former appearance. He is no longer hideous to see; he is like the gods who inhabit the vast skies. Seeing him enter the hut, Telemachus cannot believe his eyes: How can an old beggar turn into a god? Odysseus reveals his identity, but his son refuses to believe him without some proof. Odysseus gives him none, except for scolding him as a father does a son.

"Will you stop this? You've got your father right in front of you and you don't recognize him?" Of course Telemachus cannot recognize him because he's never seen him. "I tell you I am Odysseus."

By forcing the issue this way, Odysseus takes his position as father in relation to Telemachus. Until now Telemachus was in no particular position as anything, because he is not yet a man but no longer a child either, because he is dependent on his mother even as he wishes himself free: His situation is ambiguous. But with his father right there—this father he did not even know was still alive, and who may not be his father despite what he'd been told—when he sees his father standing squarely before him in flesh and blood, speaking to him as a father does to a son, not only does Odysseus feel reinforced in his identity as father, but Telemachus is finally confirmed in his identity as son. The two of them become the two terms of a social, human relationship that constitutes their identity.

With the help of Eumaeus and the cowherd, Philoetius, they determine to exact vengeance.

Meanwhile Odysseus's plan has almost been foiled: Penelope has asked to receive the old beggar whom Telemachus has mentioned and whom the nurse, Eurycleia, told her the suitors treated very shabbily. She calls him into her presence and she questions him, as she does all travelers passing through, to learn whether he has seen Odysseus. As usual, he tells her one of his lies: "Not only have I seen him—a long time ago, nearly twenty years, when he went through our parts on his way to Troy—but my brother Idomeneus went along with him to fight. I was too young myself, but I did give him lots of gifts." The queen listens to this account, wondering whether there is any truth to it. "Give me some proof of what you're saying. Can you tell me what his robe looked like?"

Of course Odysseus describes in detail the fine fabric and particularly a precious ornament that Penelope had given him, a chiseled stone showing a darting fawn. Penelope says to herself, "That's it, exactly right—he's telling the truth!" and she feels a rush of affection for this old wreck, thinking that he did after all meet Odysseus, he did help him. She asks the nurse, Eurycleia, to see to him, to bathe him and wash his feet. The nurse remarks to Penelope that the old fellow resembles Odysseus (though we might wonder how that would be possible after the metamorphosis Athena has put him through): "He has Odysseus's hands and his feet." Penelope answers, "No, not exactly: He has the hands and the feet Odysseus would have by now, after twenty years' worth of aging and suffering, if he is still alive."

Odysseus's identity is very problematic. Not only is he disguised as a beggar, but he left Ithaca at age twenty-five, so he is forty-five now. Even if his hands are the same hands, they are not identical. He is both the same and completely different.

Nonetheless the nurse claims that he resembles Odysseus, and she tells him, "Of all the people who've come through here—the travelers and the beggars who've been treated as guests and made welcome—you really are the one who most reminds me of Odysseus." "Yes, yes," says Odysseus, "I've been told that before." Then he realizes that in the course of washing his feet, Eurycleia is going to see a certain scar that will reveal his identity too soon—that could put him in an awkward position and thwart his plan.

Because when Odysseus was very young—fifteen or sixteen— he was staying at the home of his maternal grandfather for his initiation as a *kouros*—the passage from child to adult. Armed with a spear, by himself, under his cousins' surveillance, the youth was to brave a huge wild boar and bring it down—which he did, but the boar charged and it slashed open his thigh near the knee. The boy had returned very proud but with that scar, which he showed everyone; he gave detailed accounts of exactly how it had happened, how it was treated, how he'd been given gifts. Of course, as his nurse, Eurycleia had been in the front ranks listening to the story. At Odysseus's birth, when the grandfather, Autolycus, had visited, it was Eurycleia who'd put the babe on his lap, and she who'd asked him to name his grandson. One of the woman's regular tasks at the palace was to wash the feet of guests, so Eurycleia was certainly expert in all sorts of legs. Odysseus considers: "If she sees the scar, she's going to know. It will be a *sema* for her, the sign that I'm Odysseus—my signature."

He goes to sit in a dark corner hoping she will not see it. The nurse goes off to get warm water in a basin; she takes up Odysseus's foot in the dim light, her hand slides along his knee, she feels the welt, she looks closer—she drops the basin and the water spreads over the floor. She lets out a cry. Odysseus puts a hand over her mouth: She has understood. She looks toward Penelope, a look meant to tell the wife the news that this man is

Odysseus. But Athena keeps Penelope from catching the look, and from learning anything. "But Odysseus, my darling boy," murmurs Eurycleia, "however did I not recognize you right off?"

Odysseus signals her to keep silent: that though she recognizes him, Penelope must remain in ignorance. Odysseus now shows the scar to his herdsman friends as well, to prove he is who he claims to be.

STRINGING THE KING'S BOW

At Athena's instigation Penelope decides that the suitors' plundering of her household has gone on long enough. She determines to take action on the competition for her hand. Made especially lovely by the goddess's ministrations, she comes down from her room to announce to the suitors and to Odysseus, all of them humbled with admiration, that she is abandoning her longtime retirement. "If one among you is able to bend and string my husband's bow, and then to shoot through the row of targets we shall set up in the great hall, that man will become my husband and the question will be settled. And therefore preparations for the marriage ceremony—that is, decorating the house and preparing the feast—can start now." The suitors are delighted: Each of them is convinced that he will be the one who manages to string the bow. Penelope hands Eumaeus the bow and the quiverful of arrows she has taken out of their hiding place. She withdraws then and returns to her chambers. She lies down on her couch, and Athena showers her with the calm sweet sleep she yearns for.

Odysseus sees to it that the doors of the great hall are shut so that no one can leave, and that the suitors have no weapons at hand. Then begins the great bow-stringing ceremony. All the men try to bend the bow, but none can do it. Finally Antinous, the most confident contender, fails as well. Telemachus then announces that he means to try his hand, which would mean that in a sense he would be Odysseus—that thus his mother would remain with him, under his authority, and not remarry. He tries, he expects to succeed—but he too fails. Odysseus takes the bow from his hands and—still in the guise of a shabby beggar—says, "I'll have a try, too." Naturally the suitors all taunt him: "You're insane, you're out of your mind; you don't imagine you're going to marry the queen, do you?" Penelope replies that in his case it is not a question of marriage but simply of his skill at archery. Odysseus declares that of course he is not seeking to marry her, but he used to be a good shot and would like to see if he can still do it. "You're insulting us all," the suitors protest. But Penelope insists, "No, let him go ahead; if he manages—this fellow who saw my husband young—I'll give him some fine rewards, I'll give him a home or the means to go elsewhere; I'll take him out of his sorry beggar's state; I'll set him up nicely." Never for a moment does she think he might be a husband for her. Without waiting to watch, she returns to the women's quarters.

Odysseus takes up the bow, he strings it with little effort, shoots an arrow and kills one of the suitors—Antinous—to the utter stupefaction of the others. They cry out, furious, that this madman is a clumsy oaf, a public menace, he has no idea how to shoot—he didn't even aim at the target, he shot at one of them. But Odysseus goes on to kill them all, with the help of Telemachus and the two herdsmen. The suitors try to get away, but all one hundred of them are slain.

The hall is drenched with blood. Penelope, upstairs in her chambers, has seen and heard nothing of the events, because once again Athena has put her to sleep. The suitors' corpses are disposed of, the hall is washed and purified, everything is set back in order. Odysseus finds out which of the servant women have slept with the suitors and gives orders to punish them: They are strung together in a ring from the ceiling like partridges, and all of them hanged. Night falls.

The next day, there is a charade of preparing for a wedding ceremony, to keep the suitors' families from suspecting their sons' massacre: The palace is closed as if for the celebration. There is music, the whole palace resounds with the noise of the party. Eurycleia hastens up the stairs as fast as she can, to wake Penelope: "Come down—the suitors are dead, Odysseus is below!"

Penelope can hardly believe her: "If it were anyone but you telling me such wild tales, I would throw her out! Do not make light of my hopes and my pain!" The nurse insists: "I saw his scar—I recognized him, and so did Telemachus! He's killed all the suitors, I don't know how, I wasn't there, I didn't see any of it, I just heard about it!"

Penelope walks down the stairs with very mixed feelings. On the one hand she hopes that it is indeed Odysseus; at the same time she doubts that with only Telemachus's help he could have killed the hundred young warriors there. So then, this man who is supposed to be Odysseus was lying when he claimed to have encountered her husband twenty years earlier. He told her "lies as real as reality," so what proof is there that he's not still lying now? She reaches the great hall, she considers whether to run to him—but she does not move. Odysseus, still looking like an old beggar, stands before her with his eyes lowered; he says not a word. Penelope cannot speak; she is thinking that this old man is nothing at all like her Odysseus.

She is in a different position from the others. Odysseus's return puts them all back into clear-cut social position: Telemachus was in need of a father, and when Odysseus appears, he becomes his son again. Odysseus's father has a son restored to him, and the attendants the master they had been lacking: To become himself again each of them needed to regain the social relationship that underlay his role. Penelope, though, has no need of a husband—it's not a spouse she seeks, she's had a hundred of those, circling about her skirts for years now, seeking to claim that title, and irritating her no end. She does not want a husband, she wants Odysseus. She wants that man. She wants very particularly "the Odysseus of her young years." None of the signs that are convincing to other people, the public signs—the scar, the fact that he could string the bow—prove to her that this is indeed her Odysseus. Other men could offer the same signs. She wants Odysseus, which is to say, a particular person, a man who was her husband in the past long ago and who has been gone for twenty years; it's that twenty-year chasm that needs filling in. She wants some secret sign, then, a sign that only he and she could know, and there is one such thing. Penelope will have to be more cunning than Odysseus. She knows he can lie, so she will trap him.

A SECRET SHARED

Later that day Athena transforms Odysseus back into his true features: Odysseus twenty years older. He appears to Penelope then in all his beauty as a hero, and she still cannot bring herself to acknowledge him. Telemachus is furious with her. So is Eurycleia. They scold Penelope for her stony heart. But it was her tough heart that enabled her to resist everything the suitors subjected her to. "If this man is actually the one and only Odysseus, we will come back together because there is one secret absolute sign, an irrefutable sign, which only he and I know." Odysseus is all smiles;

he considers that things are going well. As the sun goes down, she craftily tells her servant women to bring out the bed from her chamber for Odysseus, for they will not spend the night together. Scarcely has she pronounced the order than Odysseus sees red, he flies into a rage: "What? Bring that bed here? But it should be impossible to move that bed!" "Why?" "Because," exclaims Odysseus, "I built that bed; I didn't make it a movable thing on four feet! The base is an olive trunk rooted in the earth! That olive tree, cut and shaped—I used that tree, still whole in the ground, to construct the couch!" At these words Penelope falls into his arms: "You are Odysseus."

That bedpost has several meanings, of course. It is fixed, immovable. The immutable nature of the base of this nuptial bed expresses the immutability of the secret the two of them share, that of her steadfastness and his identity. At the same time, this bed in which Penelope and Odysseus come together again is also the bed that confirms and consecrates the hero in his functions as king of Ithaca. The bed where the king and the queen sleep is rooted in the deepest earth of Ithaca. It represents the legitimate rights of this couple to reign over this land and to be a king and a queen of justice, connected to the fertility of the soil and of the herds. But still further, the main effect of this sign—this secret sign, whose memory they alone share and keep alive despite the passing of years—is the thing that binds them together and makes them a couple: *homophrosunē*, a commonality of thought. When Nausicaa allowed herself to mention his marriage, Odysseus told her that *homophrosunē* was the most important thing for a man and woman about to wed: that there be a harmony of thought and feeling between wife and husband. And that is what the nuptial bed represents.

This would seem to be the end, but such is not entirely the case. There is still Laertes, Odysseus's father, who has not heard about his son's return. Odysseus has a son; he has his wife, in whose gaze he can read an utter constancy; he has attendants. The story is not done until Odysseus pays a visit to his father. He has discarded his beggar's clothing, and he wants to know whether after twenty years his father will recognize him: Is Odysseus still truly himself after twenty years? He goes into the garden where his father has withdrawn—alone, unhappy, working the soil with two slave men and one slave woman. Laertes is in the same condition the dog Argus was, on his pile of dung, and as Odysseus himself was when he came to the palace as a beggar. Odysseus arrives; Laertes asks what he has come for. Odysseus begins by babbling lies: "I'm a foreigner. . . ." Talking away, he pretends to mistake his father for a slave. "You're really filthy as a dog, your clothes are so ragged, what disgusting skin, that hat's something a stable boy would wear." Laertes does not bridle at being talked to this way; he has only one question in mind: Has this traveler from abroad any news of his son?

Odysseus starts, as usual, telling him a bunch of long boring stories. Laertes bursts into tears. "Is he dead?" and takes up a handful of earth to crumble onto his head.

Seeing him in such distress, Odysseus feels he has lied enough. "Stop, Laertes—I am Odysseus!"

"What do you mean? Prove it!"

Odysseus shows him the scar, but that does not suffice for his father. Then he recounts how, when he was a very small boy, his young father, Laertes, showed and named and then gave him all these trees standing full-grown before them here in the garden now: There were thirteen pear, ten apple, and forty fig trees, and fifty rows of wine grapes. He recites every detail of the knowledge Laertes passed on to him for cultivating the earth, for growing plants and trees. In tears—of joy this time—Laertes falls into Odysseus's arms: The man who had been like a derelict feels himself King Laertes once again. Just as Odysseus had stepped into the position of father in relation to Telemachus, now he takes that of little boy to Laertes. The effect is prompt: Laertes goes into his house, and when he emerges he is grand as a god. Athena has helped things along. When he reenters the social relationship that unites him with his son, he becomes again what he used to be—regally handsome, like a god.

THE PRESENT REDISCOVERED

In the palace, in the city, the olive-trunk bedpost sunk in the heart of the household and into the land of Ithaca, in the garden, in the countryside—all that vegetation continuously maintained is what makes for the bond between past and present. The trees planted long ago have grown tall. Like unimpeachable witnesses, they mark the continuity between the time when Odysseus was a small boy and the time now, when he stands at the threshold of old age. In listening to this story, don't we do the same thing—don't we connect the past, Odysseus's departure, to the present time of his return? We weave together his separation from Penelope and his reunion with her. In a way time is annulled by memory, even as it is being retraced in the course of narration. Both annulled and represented by it, because Odysseus himself never abandoned the memory of the return, and because Penelope never abandoned the memory of the Odysseus of her own young years.

Odysseus retires to their chamber with Penelope, and it is like the first night of their marriage: They meet again as newlyweds. Athena causes the sun's chariot to stop in its tracks so that day does not break too soon, and dawn holds back. This night is the longest that ever was. The pair talk together, they tell each other their adventures and their hardships. All is now as it was long ago; time seems to fall away. The next morning the suitors' families learn of the slaughter; they cry vengeance, and a cohort of parents, brothers, cousins, kinsmen, and allies arrives with weapons in hand to battle Odysseus, Telemachus, Laertes, and their faithful attendants. Athena heads off the confrontation. There is to be no combat; truce, peace, harmony return. At Ithaca all is back as it was: There are a king and a queen; there is a son, a father, attendants; order returns. The bard's song can celebrate—for all men of all times and in all its glory—the memory of the return.

Dionysus at Thebes

In the Greek pantheon Dionysus is a god unlike any other. He is a roving, itinerant god, a god of no place and of every place. At the same time, he demands full acknowledgment wherever he passes through; he must have his position, his prestige; and since he was born in Thebes, he is particularly concerned to confirm his following there. He enters the city as a person arriving from afar—a strange stranger. He returns to Thebes, his birthplace, expecting to be welcomed, accepted—to have a kind of official headquarters there. Both itinerant and established at once, among the Greek gods he represents—as Professor Louis Gernet puts it—the figure of the other, of what is different, unsettling, disconcerting, anomic. He is also, as my colleague Marcel Detienne has written, "an epidemic god": Like a contagious disease, when he erupts in a place that has had little exposure to him, he makes quick inroads and his worship spreads like a flood.

Suddenly otherness—the other-than-oneself—asserts its presence in the most familiar places: an epidemic disease. Both itinerant and settled, he is a god close to men; his connection with them is different in nature from the sort that generally prevails in Greek religion—a bond far more intimate, more personalized, closer. Dionysus establishes a kind of direct, face-to-face relationship with his disciple; he looks deep into the disciple's eyes, and the latter in turn fastens his hypnotized gaze on the face, the mask, of Dionysus. And yet even with this closeness between him and men, he may be the god most remote from humans, the most inaccessible and mysterious, the one who cannot be apprehended, cannot be assigned to a slot. One might for instance say of Aphrodite that she is the goddess of love; of Athena that she is the goddess of war and of knowledge; of Hephaestus that he is an artisan, a blacksmith. But Dionysus cannot be put in a pigeonhole. He is simultaneously in none and in all of them, present and absent at once. The stories about him take on a somewhat special meaning when we consider the tension between vagabondage, roving, the circumstance of being always on the road, passing through, a traveler— and the circumstance of wanting a home of one's own, where one is properly settled, where one is more than accepted: chosen.

EUROPA THE WANDERER

The whole story starts with a character we already mentioned: Cadmus, the first ruler of Thebes. Cadmus, the founding hero of that great classical city, is himself a foreigner—an Asian, a Phoenician, come from afar. He is the son of Agenor, king of Tyre or Sidon, and of his queen, Telephassa. These are people from the Middle East, from what is now Syria. This royal couple, these rulers of Tyre, have a string of sons: Cadmus and his brothers Phoenix, Cilix, and Thasus; and a daughter, Europa.

Europa, a splendid young virgin, is playing with her companions on the seacoast of Tyre. Zeus looks down from high in the skies and sees her bathing, perhaps naked; she is not busy gathering bouquets as in some tales from other cultures, in which her female counterparts rouse the gods' desire by their beauty as they pluck their hyacinths or lilies or narcissus. Europa is standing in a meadow by the seashore. Zeus sees her and immediately covets her. He turns himself into a magnificent bull with horns like crescent moons. He appears on the shore and comes to lie at Europa's feet at the edge of the strand. At first rather uneasy, intimidated by the magnificent beast, Europa approaches slowly. His mild behavior gives her every reason to trust him. She strokes his head a little, pets his flanks, and when he does not move and even turns his head slightly toward her, almost licking her white skin, she sits on his broad back, takes his horns in her hands—and suddenly the bull dashes off, leaps into the water, and crosses the sea.

Zeus and the traveling Europa go from Asia to Crete. There Zeus mates with Europa and, their union consummated, he more or less settles her in Crete. She bears children—Rhadamanthus and Minos—who will be kings of Crete. Zeus presents the masters of the island with a gift: a curious figure, Talos—a kind of bronze giant whose function is to stand guard over Crete, to turn the place into a kind of fortress, a lonely island remote from the rest of the world—who both keeps any outsider from landing there and keeps the islanders from escaping to the outside. Three times a day Talos makes the rounds of the island as a watchman, preventing anyone from landing or leaving. He is immortal, invincible, ironlike. He has just one weak spot, on his heel, where a kind

of vein is fitted with a key bolt that holds it closed. All his metallic vigor will flow away if that bolt is opened. It might be the sorceress Medea who manages to open the bolt by witchcraft, during
the Argonauts' expedition; or it might be another hero, Heracles,
who at some point wounds Talos with an arrow at that vital spot,
and kills him.

Anyhow, Europa's story already puts us within a framework
involving an abduction, a movement from one world to another,
and a sequestering effect for Crete as it closes in on itself. Rather
than "movement" one might even say "wanderings": When King
Agenor learns from the girl's friends that Europa has been kid-
napped by a bull, he orders his wife and sons to find their sister
and daughter, warning them not to return home unless they bring
the girl back with them. So the three brothers and the mother set
off and begin their own roaming, leaving the place of their birth
and of their family, leaving behind their royal status, and scatter-
ing throughout the wide world. In the course of these ceaseless
peregrinations, they will establish a string of settlements. Cadmus
travels with his mother, Telephassa, and ultimately finds his way
to Thrace, still seeking his sister Europa. Telephassa dies in
Thrace, much honored.

Cadmus then goes to Delphi to inquire what he should do.
The oracle tells him: "End your wanderings; you must stop and
settle somewhere, for you will never find your sister." Europa has
disappeared; she is a wayfarer whose whereabouts no one knows.
(She is actually locked away in Crete, but who would know that
except for the Delphic oracle?) Yet the oracle does go on to say:
"You must follow after a certain cow, a wanderer herself, wherever she may go. Europa was carried off by a roaming bull who
has settled somewhere. Now you—follow after that cow, and for
as long as she walks, you must trail her; but the day she lies down
and does not rise up again, then you shall found a city there in that

place, and put down your own roots—you, Cadmus, man of Tyre." And Cadmus sets out to do as he is told, together with a few young boys. They see an especially beautiful cow, with moon markings that destine her to a special role. They follow the beast as it roams into Boeotia and then comes to a halt on a meadow— the location of the future city of Thebes. The vagabond beast moves no more, the wandering is done. Cadmus understands that this is the place where he is to build a city.

THE FOREIGNER AND THE NATIVES

But before he does so, Cadmus must make a sacrifice to Athena, a goddess he feels close to. The sacrifice requires water. He sends his companions to fill their ewers and basins at a pool called Ares' Spring, after its patron god. But the spring is guarded by a dragon, a very fierce serpent who kills all the youths who come to draw water from it. Cadmus goes himself to the spring and kills the dragon. Athena commands him to carry out the promised sacrifice and then to collect the teeth of the slaughtered dragon sprawled on the ground and sow them in a very flat plain, a *pedion*, as if they were seeds for a cereal crop. Cadmus does as instructed: He brings back the water, reverently he sacrifices the cow to Athena, then goes into the flatland and sows the dragon's teeth. Hardly has he finished than from each tooth springs up a warrior—already full grown and armed in military gear, with helmet, shield, sword, lance, leg guards, and breastplate. Once up and out of the ground, they eye one another with contempt, snarl, and hurl challenges the way men do who live for slaughter, warfare, and belligerent violence—soldiers through and through. Cadmus understands that they could easily turn on him. He therefore seizes a stone and, as the soldiers defiantly stare one another down, tosses it into their midst. Each of them thinks one of the others threw the rock, and war breaks out among them. They kill one another off—all but five. These warriors are called the Spartoi—the word means the "sown men." They are born from this soil, autochthons—true natives. These are not vagabonds; rooted in the local soil, they represent the fundamental bond with that Theban earth, and they are utterly dedicated to the warrior function. They bear names that describe them quite well: Chthonius, Oudaius, Pelorus, Hyperenor, Echion—earthy, monstrous, dark, somber, and warlike.

Still, Cadmus is the focus of Ares' rage and resentment for his having killed the dragon, who may have been Ares' son. For seven years Cadmus must go into servitude to Ares, just as in other circumstances Heracles is indentured to persons or heroes or gods he has offended. After seven years Cadmus is set free. The gods who favor him—Athena for instance—mean to install him as sovereign of Thebes. But before that can happen, this foreigner must found a family line—this man who brought to light those deep-rooted, autochthonous qualities the Theban earth harbored in its depths. At Cadmus's wedding gods and men again find themselves drawn temporarily closer. He is marrying a goddess, Harmonia, a daughter of Aphrodite and of Ares—of the very god he had to serve to expiate the crime of killing the dragon, and who still guarded and barred access to the Theban fountain, the water springing from the earth: That same warlike spirit returns and lives again through the Spartoi and their family line of creatures "born from the local soil"—of *gēgenēs*.

But through her mother, Aphrodite, his wife, Harmonia, is the goddess of union—of agreement, compatibility, reconciliation. All the gods come to the Thebes citadel to celebrate this wedding in which the bride is one of their own. The Muses chant the wedding hymn. The gods, by custom, present gifts. Some of the gifts are evil, meant to bring trouble on those who inherit them down the line. Cadmus will have several children—Semele, Autonoë, and Ino, who later becomes Leucothea, the sea goddess. Agave, another daughter, marries one of the Spartoi, Echion, and bears him a son called Pentheus. In other words, the origins of Thebes represent a balance and a union between a person from afar—Cadmus—become ruler by virtue of his exploits and by the will of the gods, and on the other side, persons entrenched in the land, sprung from the soil, autochthons—natives who have the Theban earth stuck to their sandal soles and who are warriors pure and simple. The early sequence of Theban kings continually gives rise to the feeling that between these two lines—these two forms of breeding—there ought to be harmony, but there can also be tensions, misunderstandings, and conflicts.

THE UTERINE THIGH

One of Cadmus's daughters, Semele, is a ravishing creature, like Europa. Zeus carries on relations with her, not briefly but fairly long term. Semele sees Zeus lie down beside her every night in human form, but she knows that it is in fact Zeus, and she wants the god to appear to her as himself, in all his brilliance, his majesty as the king of the blissful immortals. Endlessly she implores him to show himself to her. Now, of course, though the gods may occasionally come to humans' celebrations, it can be dangerous for men to ask such a being to appear to their unprotected eyes, as a mortal partner would. When Zeus yields to Semele's entreaty and appears in his thunderous splendor, Semele is consumed by the radiance and the blaze, the divine brilliance of her lover. She burns to ash. She is already pregnant with Dionysus by him; without a moment's hesitation Zeus lifts little Dionysus out of Semele's body as it burns, slashes his own thigh, spreads the wound, converts his thigh into a female womb, and sets the six-month fetus inside it. Thus Dionysus is doubly Zeus's son—he is called "the twice-born": When the time comes Zeus reopens his thigh, and the infant Dionysus emerges the same way he was taken from Semele's belly. The child is bizarre, abnormal from the standpoint of the gods, since he is simultaneously the son of a mortal woman and the son of Zeus in all his brilliance. He is bizarre because he was nurtured partly in a woman's belly and partly in Zeus's thigh. Dionysus will have to battle the unrelenting jealousy of Hera, who does not easily forgive Zeus his peccadilloes, and who always resents the fruits of his clandestine amours. One of Zeus's major concerns is therefore to keep Dionysus out of Hera's sight, entrusting him to nurses who'll hide him.

He isn't much older when he too starts roaming the earth, and often finds himself persecuted by people comfortably established in their own world. While still quite young, for instance, he lands in Thrace with his retinue of young Bacchae—his worshipers—at his heels. The king of the land, Lycurgus, takes a very sour view of the arrival of this young foreigner, coming from who knows where, claiming to be a god, and these young women raving as fanatical followers of a new divinity. Lycurgus has the Bacchae arrested and thrown into prison. Already Dionysus has power enough to get them set free. Lycurgus pursues the god and forces him to flee. An ambiguous, questionable deity, what with his effeminate strain, Dionysus panics at the chase: He finally leaps into the water to escape Lycurgus. The sea nymph Thetis, Achilles' future mother, hides him for a time down in the depths of the ocean. When he emerges from that episode—a kind of secret initiation—he disappears from Greece and heads for Asia. And then comes the great conquest of Asia. He roams all those territories with armies of the faithful—women mainly, who are not armed with the warrior's classic weapons but who fight with blows from a thyrsus, a long pointed staff with a pine cone attached; the wand has supernatural powers. Dionysus and his disciples scatter the many armies that attack him in a vain effort to block his advance; he moves through Asia as a conqueror. Then the god turns back to Greece.

ITINERANT PRIEST AND WILD WOMEN

Now for his return to Thebes. The wanderer, the little child pursued by a bitter stepmother's hatred, the young god obliged to leap into the water and hide in the watery deeps to escape the fury of a Thracian king—now as an adult he turns back to Thebes. The present king is his cousin Pentheus. The son of Agave, sister to Dionysus's mother, Semele, Pentheus succeeded to the throne after their common grandfather, Cadmus, who is still living but too old to reign. His father was Echion, one of the five Spartoi warriors sprung of the earth-sown dragon teeth; from him Pentheus inherited his deep connection with the Theban soil, his roots in the place, his violent temperament, his soldierly intransigence and arrogance.

The city of Thebes is something of a model archaic Greek city; Dionysus comes to it in disguise. He presents himself not as the god Dionysus but as the god's priest. An itinerant priest, clothed as a woman, wearing his long hair down his back, he is the compleat Eastern half-breed, with his dark eyes, his seductive look, his smooth talk—all the features that could infuriate and raise the hackles of that "sown man" from Theban soil, Pentheus. The two are roughly the same age. Pentheus is a very young king, and this so-called priest is a very young god. Around the priest swarms a whole band of women, younger and older, who are Lydians, women of the East—the East as a physical type, as a way of being. They make a racket in the streets of the city, they sit about and eat and sleep out in the open air. Pentheus sees all this and goes into a rage. What is this bunch of strays doing here? He wants to put them out. And all the Theban matrons whom Dionysus has turned mad because he does not forgive his mother's sisters—Cadmus's other daughters, especially Agave—for claiming that Semele never had any liaison with Zeus, that she was a hysteric who'd had flings with who knows who, that she'd died in a fire through her own carelessness, and that if she did have a son, he had disappeared; in any case he couldn't be by Zeus. That whole segment of the family saga that Semele represented, the fact that she did sustain the long relationship with the world of the gods, even if she was wrong to want too much from the liaison— the Thebans deny it all: They just find the story a big bore. Yes, there was the wedding of Cadmus and Harmonia, granted, but that was about establishing a human city organized according to proper human criteria. Dionysus, however, is seeking to reestablish a connection to the divine, although a different sort from the wedding of Cadmus and Harmonia. Reestablish it not just for the occasion of some festival, some ceremony where the gods decide to come by and then leave, but in actual human life—in the political and civic life of Thebes as it is. He means to introduce a ferment that opens up a new dimension in the daily existence of every single person. To do that he has to madden the women of Thebes, those matrons solidly established in their position of wife and mother, whose way of life is at the very farthest extreme from the Lydians who make up Dionysus's entourage. Such are the Theban women the god has driven into a frenzy.

They desert their children, abandon their household tasks,

leave their husbands, and take off into the mountains, into the wilderness, into the woods. There they run about in garb that is startling for women of dignity, they indulge in all sorts of insanities while the peasants look on with mixed feelings—stunned, admiring, and shocked at the same time. Pentheus is informed of all this. His fury mounts. First he turns against the followers, the god's devotees; he blames them for the female chaos spreading through the city. He commands his police to seize all the fervent Lydian women of the new cult, and throw them into prison—this from the urban law-and-order officials. No sooner are they jailed than Dionysus frees them by magic. They are out again, dancing and singing in the streets, clacking their rattles, making a racket. Pentheus decides to attack this rootless priest, this seductive beggar. He orders him arrested, shackled, and locked up in the royal stables with the livestock, the cows and horses. The priest is led away, completely unresisting, smiling and calm, a little ironical and passive. He is jailed in the royal stables. Pentheus considers that the problem is solved, and instructs his men to prepare for a military expedition—to go out into the countryside to chase down and bring in all those women carrying on with their wild doings out there. The soldiers form columns four abreast and march out of the city, where they'll scatter over the fields and woods and surround the group of women.

Meanwhile Dionysus is still in his stable. But suddenly his chains fall away, and the royal palace bursts into flames. The walls crumble, and he leaves unharmed. Pentheus is badly shaken, especially since just as these events occur and he sees his palace collapse, suddenly that same priest appears before him, still smiling, unhurt, thoroughly shabby, and gazing at him. His chiefs arrive, bloody, disheveled, their armor shattered. "What's happened to you all?" They explain, as in a military report: As long as those women were left undisturbed, they seemed perfectly happy, not in

the least aggressive or threatening—quite the contrary: Within themselves, among them and around them, out in the meadows and in the forests, everything was marvelously gentle, kindly; you'd see them pick up baby animals, every kind of animal, and nurse them at their breasts like their own babes, and never did these wild beasts they were handling do them the slightest harm. According to reports from the peasants, and from the soldiers' own observations too, the women were living as if in a world apart, a return to perfect harmony among all living creatures, men and beasts mingling together—wild animals, predatory carnivores, at peace with their prey, side by side, all full of delight in the same spirit, and with frontiers gone, in friendship and peace. The earth itself joined as one with them; at the light touch of their thyrsus, fountains of pure water or milk or wine would spring from the soil—the return of the golden age. But the moment the soldiers appear, the moment military violence touches them, these angelic women turn into murderous furies. With those same thyrsi they stampeded the soldiers, broke through their ranks, beat them, killed them—it was a total rout. A victory of gentleness over violence, of women over men, of the wild countryside over civic order. . . .

Pentheus learns of the debacle as Dionysus stands smiling before him. Pentheus embodies the Greek man in one of his major aspects: convinced that what counts is a certain aristocratic form—of behavior, of self-control, of reasoning ability. And then further, the self-imposed determination never to commit a base act, to know how to govern oneself and not be a slave to one's desires or passions—an attitude whose corollary involves a certain contempt for women, who by contrast are viewed as yielding easily to emotion. And contempt as well for everything not Greek: for the Barbarians from Asia, lascivious people whose skin is too white because they don't exercise in the stadium, who are unwill-

ing to endure the hardships required to attaining that self-mastery. In other words, Pentheus harbors the idea that a monarch's role is to uphold a hierarchical system in which men take their proper place, women stay home, foreigners are not let in, and Asia— the East—is considered to be populated by effeminate folk in the habit of obeying a tyrant's orders, whereas Greece is populated by free men.

Standing face to face with Pentheus, this young priest is in a way his portrait and his double: They are first cousins, the same age, of the same family, both natives of Thebes, even though one has a whole nomadic history behind him. If one were to lift away from Pentheus that kind of carapace—that shell or covering he's constructed so as to feel himself truly a man, an *aner*, a man who knows his duty to himself and his duty to the community, forever prepared when called upon to command and to punish—underneath it one would find none other than Dionysus.

"I SAW HIM SEEING ME"

Dionysus, the "priest," proceeds with a sophist's shrewd style—by questions and by ambiguous answers—to rouse Pentheus's curiosity about what goes on in a world he does not know and has no wish to know: that unruly female world. In the *gynaeceum* a person has at least some rough idea what women do—it's never completely clear what they're up to, those she-devils, but generally they are under some surveillance. But out there on their own, no longer in the city, away from among the temples and streets where everything is under close scrutiny—out there in the wild, with no witnesses, who knows how far they go? Pentheus would like to know, though. In his dialogue with Dionysus, Pentheus gradually comes to ask: "Who is this god? How is it you know him? You've seen him? At night in a dream?"

"No, no, I've seen him when I'm wide awake," answers the priest. "I saw him seeing me. I've watched him watching me."

Pentheus wonders what the phrase means, "I saw him seeing me."

This idea of looking, of the eye—that there are things one cannot know but knows better if one sees them—little by little this idea germinates in the brain of the establishment man, the city dweller, the monarch—the Greek. He decides that it might not be a bad thing to go out and see. He is manifesting a desire he did not know he had: the desire to be a voyeur. All the more because he believes that as they abandon themselves to anarchy out in the countryside, these women—women of his own family—are indulging in hair-raising sexual orgies. He is prudish—as a wifeless young man, he probably keeps a very tight rein on himself in this area—but the whole business excites him, he is eager to see what does go on out there. The "Dionysian priest" tells him, "Easily arranged: Your soldiers got run out because they arrived with their weapons and in columns four abreast; they just presented themselves in plain sight. But you—you can go out there without anyone seeing you, in secret; you can watch their frenzy, their madness, you'll have a front-row seat and no one will see you. All you need to do is dress like me."

So suddenly the king—this citizen, this Greek, this male—dresses up like Dionysus's roving priest: He puts on women's clothing, he lets his hair loose, he feminizes himself, he becomes like that Asian. At one point, as they stand face to face, they seem to be looking at themselves in a mirror, each at each, eye to eye. Dionysus takes Pentheus by the hand and leads him out to Mount Cithaeron where the women are camped. One behind the other, the man rooted in the local soil—the man with an identity and the one who comes from afar, the embodiment of the other—walk together away from the city, toward the mountain, toward the slopes of Cithaeron.

The priest points out a very tall pine tree and tells Pentheus to climb it and hide in the branches: From there the king will be able to observe everything; he will see and not be seen. Pentheus clambers to the top of the pine. Perched up there he waits; then he sees his mother, Agave, arrive with all the Theban women Dionysus has unhinged, who are in an odd state of delirium as a result. He has unhinged them, yes, but they are not truly his followers, not "converts" to the Dionysian cult. On the contrary: Agave and the other women insist that all this is not really happening. Despite themselves, this madness, which is not the effect of a conviction or a religious conversion, seems more like the symptom of some sickness. From not fully accepting the faith, not believing in it, they are sick from it; in the face of unbelief, the Dionysus fervor comes out as a contagious disease. In their madness at times they are like votaries of the god, beatific over the return to a golden age of brotherhood in which all living beings—gods and men and beasts—live together. And at other times they are seized by bloodthirsty rage; just as they slashed the army to shreds, they could cut their own children's throats, or do anything else. The Theban women are in this hallucinatory state of derangement, of "dionysiac epidemic."

Dionysus is not yet established in the city; he has not been accepted, he is still that outsider whom people look at askance. Perched high up in his pine tree, Pentheus watches the women scattered through the woodland. They are going about the peaceable activities that are their custom as long as no one is hunting them, persecuting them. Then at a certain point, in an effort to see better, Pentheus leans out a little too far, and the women catch sight of a spy, of a lookout, a voyeur up there. They fly into an instant fury and rush over to try to bend the tree down. They cannot, and they attempt to uproot it instead. Pentheus starts swaying dangerously at the top of the tree, and he shouts, "Mother, it's me, it's Pentheus! Watch out, you'll make me fall!" But frenzy has already possessed them utterly, and they do manage to buckle the tree. Pentheus topples to the ground, they fall on him and shred him to pieces. They rip him apart the way the victim animal would be ripped apart raw and alive in some Dionysian rites of sacrifice—Pentheus is dismembered in the same way. His mother snatches up her son's severed head, sticks it on the tip of a thyrsus, and marches about in delight with the thing, which in her delirium she imagines to be the head of a young lion or bull impaled on the end of her pike. She is wildly happy. Since even in her Dionysiac frenzy she is still what she is—the daughter of Echion, a woman of a warrior breed—she boasts of having been hunting with the men and like a man, of showing herself to be even better at hunting than they. With that mob of demented, blood-spattered women, Agave goes over to Dionysus, who is still garbed as a priest.

With him are old Cadmus, the founder of Thebes, Agave's father and thus the grandfather of Pentheus, to whom he had ceded the throne; and Tiresias, the venerable seer who in the townsfolk's mind represents the everyday wisdom of old age, a rather ritualistic wisdom. Neither of them cares to get much involved with Dionysus, but still, neither do they feel that virulent hostility to him, that utter hatred—Cadmus because he is Cadmus, and because he is also the father of Semele, Dionysus's mother; Tiresias because his function is to establish the link with heaven. But also they both feel a kind of cautious fascination. And so they have decided—despite their great age and their difficulties in following the action—to put on the ritual costume, the floating garments like everyone else, and to pick up a thyrsus, to join the women out in the forests and dance with them, as if the business of honoring the god recognized no distinctions of age or gender. So these two old fellows are present when Agave in her frenzy comes brandishing Pentheus's head atop her thyrsus. Agave sees

Cadmus and shows off her splendid catch; she boasts that she is the best hunter in the city, even better than the men. "Look, I hunted these wild beasts and I killed them!" Horrified at the sight, Cadmus seeks to bring her slowly back to her senses, questioning her very gently: "What's happened? Look at this lion's head, look at the hair—don't you recognize them?" Little by little Agave emerges from her delirium. Slowly fragments of reality reappear in that dreamlike universe, at once bloody and gorgeously beautiful, in which she was foundering. . . . Finally she understands that the head spiked on her thyrsus is her son's. The horror!

THE REJECTION OF THE OTHER, AND LOST IDENTITY

Dionysus's return to his home in Thebes ran up against a failure of understanding, and caused conflict for as long as the city remained incapable of forging some connection between the local citizens and the stranger—between those who stay put and the wanderers; between the city's will to keep being what it is, to preserve its identity, reject change, on the one hand and on the other the outsider, the alien, the other. So long as there is no possibility of reconciling these opposites, a terrifying thing occurs: Those who embodied the unconditional attachment to the unchanging, who proclaimed the need to preserve traditional values against whatever is other from themselves, against whatever questions them or forces them to see themselves differently—these "identitarians," the Greek citizens confident of their superiority—are the very ones who topple over into absolute otherness, into horror, into the monstrous. The Theban women, for instance, so irreproachable in behavior, models of reserve and modesty in their domestic life, all of them—Agave foremost, the queen mother who kills her son and tears him to pieces and brandishes his head like a trophy—all of them suddenly become like the dreaded Gorgon Medusa: Their eyes carry death. Pentheus dies hideously, ripped apart alive like a wild animal—Pentheus, the civilized man, the ever self-controlled Greek, who yielded to the fascination of what he had considered to be the other and had condemned. The horror comes to cast itself onto the face of the very person who could not make room for the other.

After these events Agave goes into exile, as does Cadmus, and Dionysus continues his travels through the world, with his status in heaven assured. He will have a congregation right there in Thebes; he has conquered the city—not to force out the other gods, not to impose his religion as against the others, but so that the marginal and the nomadic, the alien, the anomic, should have a presence in the center of Thebes, at the city's heart, by way of his temple, his feast-days, his worship. It is as if insofar as one human group refuses to acknowledge the other, to grant it a share, the first group becomes monstrously other itself.

Dionysus's return home to Thebes recalls the accord with the world of the gods that had been sealed, rather ambiguously even at the time, in the town citadel when all the gods gave Cadmus his wife, Harmonia, daughter of Ares and Aphrodite. That moment held perhaps not the promise but at least the possibility of a world reconciled—and also the eventuality at any time of a breach, of division and massacre. This is common knowledge—the Dionysus story is not the only evidence; Cadmus is the god's grandfather, but he is also ancestor to the House of Labdacus, which proves that the best and the worst can occur together. The Labdacid legend ends with the story of Oedipus; in it we also see the constant tension between those who are true kings and others who, even within the kingship, draw far more on the family line of the "sown men," those legendary warrior Spartoi bent on violence and hatred.

Oedipus Out of Joint

After Pentheus's tragic death Cadmus and Agave left Thebes, and both the throne and the city's whole system were in great disarray. Who was to be king? Who would embody a king's virtues, and his ability to rule? The succession would normally pass to Cadmus's other son, Polydorus; he is wed to the daughter of a "sown man," Chthonius—the man of the local soil, of the underground. Her name is Nicteis—shadowed, nocturnal; she is the sister or the near relative of a whole series of figures—for instance Nicteus and Lycus (the wolf)—connected to the *gēgēnēs*, those earth-sown men who stand for violence of war.

Pentheus himself had a double lineage. His mother, Agave, was the daughter of Cadmus, founder of Thebes, so he is descended from the true sovereign designated by the gods, from the ruler

the gods gifted with a goddess as his wife as if to mark the nature
of his kingly power. Then he also belonged to that tribe of sown
men through his father, Echion. (The name has a "viprous" over-
tone, for it readily calls to mind a female figure, Echidna—half
woman, half serpent, sister to the Gorgons, an "irresistible monster lurking in the secret depths of the earth"—who gives birth to
disasters like Hades' dog Cerberus, and the three-headed Chimera,
whom Bellerophon kills with the help of Pegasus the horse.) So
Pentheus is torn between Cadmus's regal heritage and those other
earth-born characters with their dark, monstrous nature.

After Pentheus's hideous death, then, the throne stands
vacant. Polydorus occupies it only very briefly; he was supposed
to pass the throne to his son Labdacus ("the lame")—a legitimate
son but whose lineage is actually "lame," or defective, because
while through his father he descends directly from Cadmus and
the goddess Harmony, his mother, Nicteis, links him to those violent warrior Spartoi. At his father's death, though, Labdacus is too
young to assume the duties of a king, and a regent takes the
throne.

So the early stages of that Theban state are unstable, racked. It
is a time of violence, of disorder, of usurpation, during which,
instead of passing from father to son in a steady and predictable
succession, the throne jumps from one hand to the next amid struggles and rivalries that set the Spartoi against one another and
against the legitimate royal power. Labdacus rules for a while, but
when he in turn dies, his son, Laius, is barely a year old, and once
again the throne stands empty. Nicteus and Lycus take it over. They
hold it a long while, Lycus in particular—eighteen years, according
to the sparse information. Throughout this time, young Laius is
still incapable of exercising sovereignty. Lycus and Nicteus are both
ousted by persons foreign to Thebes, Amphion and Zethus, who
eventually return the throne to Laius as the legitimate heir.

Until then, though, for as long as the usurpers manage to keep him out of power, Laius is forced to live in exile. He is already an adult when he finds refuge at Corinth with King Pelops, who generously extends him hospitality and keeps him close.

LAME GENERATIONS

Here in the story comes an episode with important consequences. In Corinth, Laius falls in love with Pelops's son Chrysippe, a very beautiful young man. He courts the boy assiduously, takes him around on his chariot, behaves as an older man toward a younger one—he teaches him to be a man; at the same time, though, he seeks an erotic relationship with him, and the king's son refuses. Laius may even have tried to obtain by force what seduction and merit could not get him. According to the story, too, in his anger and shock Chrysippe kills himself. Whatever the case, Pelops pronounces a solemn curse upon Laius—that his line, the House of Labdacus, shall not survive—that it shall be doomed to annihilation.

The name Labdacus means "lame," and the meaning of Laius's own name is unclear; it could mean "leader of a people," or a "gauche—clumsy—man." It's worth noting, in fact, that all Laius's relationships are awkward or mishandled. For one thing, from the standpoint of the royal succession: That should have come down directly to him from his father, Labdacus, his grandfather, Polydorus, and his great-grandfather Cadmus, and set him solidly on the Theban throne. Yet he was put aside, turned away, distanced from it: So the succession was thrown off course. Another deviation with Laius: At the age when he ought to be thinking of taking a wife, he turns to this young boy. But most important, he fouls the game of love, by looking to impose by force something that Chrysippe was unwilling to offer him spontaneously; between them there was a lack of reciprocity, of *charis*—grace—of equitable amorous exchange. The one-sided erotic urge is stymied. Furthermore, Laius is Pelops's guest, and the guest-host relationship calls for reciprocity of friendship, of gifts back and forth. But far from repaying his host for welcoming him, Laius attempts to take his son against the boy's will, provoking his suicide.

Lycus had been ruling Thebes; he was replaced by Amphion and Zethus, who also die. Laius returns to the city, and the Thebans are very glad to welcome him and to entrust the throne again to a person they see as worthy of it.

Laius marries Jocasta. She too is strongly linked by descent to the "sown man" Echion: She is the great-granddaughter of that figure who—like Chthonius—represents the dark and somber heritage. As per Pelops's curse, the marriage of Laius and Jocasta is childless. Laius goes to Delphi to ask the oracle what he should do to produce descendants, so that the path of succession might return to a straight line at last. The oracle answers: "If you have a son, he will kill you and he will bed his mother." Laius returns to Thebes in horror. Thereafter his sexual relations with his wife are such as to ensure that she will not bear a child, not become pregnant. But, the story goes, one day Laius drinks too much, and he mindlessly plants his wife's furrow—to speak like the Greeks—with a seed that goes on to sprout. Jocasta gives birth to a boy. In view of the prediction, the couple determine to set aside, break off the family line and arrange for the infant to die. They call in one of their herdsmen, who go each summer up onto Mount Cithaeron to pasture the royal flocks. He is ordered to take the child—and expose him on the mountainside to be devoured by wild beasts or birds.

The herdsman takes the newborn babe, pierces a hole through his heel, slips a thong through it, and goes off carrying the child on his back as if he were some small game from the hunt. He reaches the mountain with his flocks, and the infant smiles at him. He hesitates—must he desert him here? He no longer thinks he can do it. He sees a shepherd from Corinth grazing his animals on the next slope. He asks the fellow to take this child, whom he cannot bring himself to leave to die. The shepherd thinks of his own King Polybius and Queen Periboea of Corinth, who have no child and who long for one. So he takes them the baby with the wounded heel: "Oedipus," the swollen-footed. Delighted with the godsend, the two rulers raise him as if he were their own son. This child—the grandson of Labdacus the Lame, the son of Laius, who was himself shut out of power and who strayed from the righteous path of the hospitality bond and of sexual relations—this little boy is thus removed, in turn, from his fatherland, his native ground, his position as a royal child carrying on the Labdacid dynasty. He is raised, he grows up, and when he becomes an adolescent, everyone admires his bearing, his courage, his intelligence. The younger generation of the Corinthian elite feel some degree of jealousy and ill will toward him.

"A BOGUS SON"

Though he does not actually limp in the true sense of the word, Oedipus does still bear on his heel the mark of his banishment, of his displacement from his rightful role, from his true origins. So he too is in a state of imbalance. As the king's son, everyone reckons him to be the designated successor to Polybius—but he is not fully a boy of Corinth; people know it, and they speak of it privately.

One day, in a squabble with a boy his own age, the other youth sneers, "Anyway, you're a bogus son!" Oedipus goes to find his father and tells him that a companion called him "bogus," as if he were not really the king's child. Polybius reassures him as best he can, without declaring categorically, "No, no, absolutely not true, you really are our son, of your mother and me!" All he says is, "That's just foolish talk, it doesn't mean a thing. Pay no attention. People are envious, they'll say all kinds of things." Oedipus is still uneasy, and he decides to go consult the oracle at Delphi to ask about his birth. Is he or is he not the son of Polybius and Periboea? The oracle takes care not to give him an answer as clear as his question. But it does say, "You shall kill your father; you shall bed your mother." Oedipus is horrified, and that dreadful revelation distracts him from his original question —"Am I the true son?" His urgent task now is to get away, to put the greatest possible distance between himself and the couple he considers to be his father and mother—to go into exile, to flee, to leave, to journey as far from Corinth as he can. And so he departs; a little like Dionysus, he becomes a wanderer. He has no soil stuck to his sandals anymore—no more fatherland. On his chariot or on foot alongside it, he leaves Delphi and takes the other road—toward Thebes.

It happens that just then the city of Thebes is suffering a terrible scourge, and King Laius has resolved to go to Delphi to ask the oracle's counsel. He leaves Thebes with a small party, in his chariot with his coachman and a few attendants. So here are the father and the son—the father convinced that his son is long dead, the son sure that his father is someone else entirely—traveling toward each other. They meet where three roads cross, a spot where it is impossible for two chariots to pull past each other. Oedipus is in his chariot, Laius in his; Laius feels that his royal retinue should have the right of way, and he has his driver signal the youth to move aside. "Get out of the way, let us by!" shouts Laius's man, and with his club he strikes one of the horses pulling Oedipus's chariot—he may even have touched Oedipus on the shoulder. Oedipus, who is not an accommodating fellow and who, even in his new role as a self-banished person, considers himself a prince, a king's son, is hardly inclined to make room for anyone. The coachman's blow infuriates him, and he raises his own crop, strikes Laius's driver, and lays him out dead; he then attacks Laius, who also falls dead at his feet, while one man of the royal entourage escapes and rushes back in terror to Thebes. Oedipus, considering that the whole thing was an ordinary travel incident and that he was acting in legitimate self-defense, goes on his way and his wandering.

He reaches Thebes much later; calamity is brooding over the city in the form of a monster—half woman, half lion, with a woman's head and breasts and the body and claws of a lion: the Sphinx. The creature is stationed at the gates of Thebes, some-times on a column, sometimes on a rock higher up. She enjoys posing riddles to the young townsmen. Every year she requires that the elite of Theban youth, the finest boys, be sent to brave her challenge; some accounts say she demands sexual congress with them. In any event she sets them her riddle, and when they cannot answer, she puts them to death. Thus, over the years, Thebes is seeing the flower of its youth slaughtered, destroyed. When Oedipus reaches Thebes and enters through one of the gates, he sees all the people in terrible distress, their expressions grim. He wonders what's going on. The regent who replaced Laius—Jocasta's brother, Creon—is also decended from the Spartoi. At the sight of this dashing young man with his bold manner, Creon says to himself that this stranger may be their last chance to save the city. He tells Oedipus that if he can beat the monster at her game, the queen will be his bride.

DIRE AUDACITY

Since Jocasta was widowed she is formally the sovereign, but Creon actually wields the power. By that authority he can promise Oedipus that if he conquers the Sphinx both the queen and the throne will be his. Oedipus confronts the Sphinx. The monster is stationed on her little mound; she sees Oedipus coming, and notes that he'll make a fine victim. She frames the following riddle: "What creature, alone among all who live upon land or in the waters or in the air, has one single voice, one way of speaking, one nature, yet goes on two feet, three feet, and four feet—*dipous, tripous, tetrapous?*"

Oedipus ponders. His pondering may come easier for a man called Oedipus; *dipous*, meaning "two-footed," is contained in his very name.

He answers, "The answer is man. As an infant, a man moves on all fours; then he stands upright on his two legs; and when he is old he leans on a cane to aid his uncertain, halting walk." Bested in this test of arcane knowledge, the Sphinx flings herself from the top of her column, or her rock, and dies.

The whole city of Thebes is delirious with happiness. Oedipus is acclaimed and borne back into the city in great pomp. He is present-ed to Queen Jocasta and wed to her as his reward. Oedipus becomes king; he has earned the position by giving proof of the greatest wis-dom and audacity. He is a worthy descendant of his grandfather Cadmus, whom the gods had honored by granting him the goddess Harmonia for his wife and appointing him founder of Thebes.

All goes well for many years. The royal couple gives birth to four children: two sons—Polynices and Eteocles, and two daughters—Ismene and Antigone. Then another plague strikes Thebes brutally.

Everything had seemed prosperous and normal and balanced; suddenly everything falls apart, everything turns to disaster. When things go as they should, each year the grain comes up again, the fruit reappears on the trees, the flocks breed sheep and goats and calves: In short the wealth of the Theban earth is renewed with the seasons. And the women too are caught up in this great freshening of the life force: They bear beautiful children, strong and healthy. Then suddenly this whole normal pattern is interrupted, thrown off kilter; it goes lame, disabled. The women miscarry or they bring forth monsters. The very wellsprings of life are tainted; they run dry. And on top of it all, some disease strikes men and women both, old and young, and kills all kinds indiscriminately. Panic spreads, Thebes is frantic—what is happening? What's gone wrong?

Creon sends an emissary to Delphi to question the oracle and find out the reason for this infectious disease, this epidemic ravaging the city and wreaking chaos. Representatives of the two extremes of Thebes's vital force—the youngest children and the most aged (the four-legged and the three-legged)—gather at the royal palace carrying ritual branches in supplication. They implore Oedipus to rescue them. "Be our savior! Once before, you spared us from disaster—delivered us from that hideous monster the Sphinx—now save us from this *loimos*, this plague on everything, not just human beings but all our plants and livestock too! As if the whole process of renewal in Thebes is choked off!"

Oedipus makes a solemn pledge to investigate; he will find out the cause of the evil and put an end to the scourge. Just then, the messenger returns from Delphi. The oracle has declared that the evil will not cease until Laius's murder is expiated: The man who has Laius's blood on his hands must be found and punished and banished from Thebes forever. Hearing this, Oedipus makes a fur-

ther solemn pledge: "I shall seek out and find the guilty one."
Oedipus is a man of inquiry, a questioner, an interrogator. Just as
he left Corinth to go wherever fortune took him, he is also a man
for whom the random adventure of thought, of questioning, is
always to be tried. There's no stopping Oedipus. So he begins an
investigation, like a police inquiry.

As a first step he puts out word that anyone with possible
information should bring it to him, and anyone who might find
himself in contact with a suspected murderer should run him out:
The murderer cannot remain in Thebes, for the city's suffering
comes from his polluting presence. Until the assassin is found and
banished from the homes and sanctuaries and streets, Oedipus will
not rest. He must know. He begins his investigation. Creon tells
the people that Thebes has a professional seer who can decode the
flight of birds, and who might perhaps find out the truth by divine
revelation: It is old Tiresias. Creon urges that he be brought in and
questioned. The old sage is not eager to appear, to be interrogat-
ed. Nonetheless he is brought onto the public square, before the
people of Thebes, before the council of elders, before Creon and
Oedipus.

Oedipus questions him, but Tiresias refuses to answer; he
claims to know nothing. Fury from Oedipus, who has no great
respect for the seer: Hadn't he been cleverer, wiser himself? He
was the one whose experience, whose judgment as a rational man,
had worked out the answer to the Sphinx's riddle; whereas
Tiresias, with all his inspiration and all his reading of omens, had
been incapable of providing it. Oedipus comes up against a wall
with him—but it is not a wall of ignorance: Tiresias is refusing to
reveal what he knows through divine wisdom. He does know
everything—who killed Laius, and who Oedipus actually is—
because he is in contact with his master, Apollo. It was Apollo,
speaking through his oracle at Delphi, who had told Oedipus,

"You shall kill your father; you shall lie with your mother." Tiresias understands how Oedipus is implicated in Thebes's misery, but he will not breathe a word of it. He is quite determined to say nothing on the subject—to the point where Oedipus, in a fury at his stubbornness, becomes convinced that the refusal cannot be mere chance: Tiresias and Creon must be plotting against him, so as to destabilize him and take over the throne. He imagines that Creon has some arrangement with Tiresias—that he may even have bribed the seer, and that the envoy sent to Delphi was in on the scheme as well.

Rage sweeps over Oedipus, he loses his head and orders Creon to leave the city instantly. He suspects him of having arranged for Laius's murder: If Creon wanted Laius dead so he could rule through his sister, Jocasta, he might have fomented the attack. Now the highest level of the state is falling to the forces of disunion, of open struggle. Oedipus wants to banish Creon, but Jocasta intervenes. She tries to restore harmony between the two men, the two family groups. These are not clearcut bloodlines, with Cadmus on one side and the Spartoi on the other; the two tribes have always been intermingled. Labdacus, Laius, and Oedipus all have some Spartoi in their background as well. As for Jocasta, she is a direct descendant of that same Echion, a figure who is dreadfully disturbing. So the city is torn apart; the leaders are battling, detesting one another, and meanwhile Oedipus pursues his investigation.

There is a firsthand witness who should be consulted—the man who was on the scene with Laius at the time of the murder, and who escaped. On his return to Thebes he had reported that a band of thugs had ambushed the royal chariot on its way to Delphi, killing Laius and the driver. When Oedipus, as examining magistrate, had first heard the account of Laius's death, he was somewhat troubled: The event had occurred where three roads cross in a narrow pass close to Delphi, and he knew that crossroads, that pass, only too well. What assuaged his concern was that, while he did not know whom he had killed, he did know he had acted alone, whereas in the story it was many men, a band of thugs, who attacked Laius. He reasons very simply: If it was a band of thugs, it wasn't me. These were two separate events: I was struck by a man in a chariot; and then there was Laius's chariot attacked by a gang. They're two completely separate stories.

Now Oedipus would like to call in the man who was present at the event, and he asks what has become of him. He is told that once he was back in Thebes, the man scarcely set foot in the city again; he has retired to the country and nobody sees him. Very strange. He must be brought in and questioned about the circumstances surrounding the attack. They bring in Laius's miserable attendant. Oedipus grills him, but the man is no more forthcoming than Tiresias was. Oedipus has enormous trouble extracting any information from him; he even threatens torture to make him talk.

Just then a stranger arrives from Corinth, after a long journey. He comes before Jocasta and Oedipus, gives greeting, asks for the king of the country. He has come to bring sad news: Oedipus's father and mother, the king and queen of Corinth, are dead. This pains Oedipus, for he is now an orphan. But it is pain mitigated by a certain rejoicing, because if Polybius is dead, Oedipus can no longer kill his father—he is deceased. Nor can he sleep with his mother, since she too has already died. Oedipus—this clear-minded, freethinking man—is not displeased to see the oracle proved wrong. To the bearer of the sorry news, who may be expecting Oedipus to return to Corinth to take up power there as provided, Oedipus explains himself: He had no choice but to quit Corinth, for it was predicted that he would kill his father and lie with his mother. The messenger replies, "But you were wrong to worry about that: Polybius and Periboea were not your father and mother." Oedipus is stunned; what can he mean?

"YOUR PARENTS WERE NOT YOUR PARENTS"

Jocasta hears the messenger explain that Oedipus was brought into the palace at Corinth as a newborn, and adopted in his early weeks by the king and queen. He was not the fruit of their loins, but they did intend that Corinth should go to him. Jocasta is struck by a terrible realization. If she had not already half guessed, all is clear to her now. She turns away from the discussion and goes into the palace.

"How do you know this?" Oedipus asks the messenger.

"I know it," he answers, "because I was the one who brought that baby to my masters. I brought you—you, the baby with the pierced heel."

"Who gave you the child?" asks Oedipus.

Among the gathering the messenger points to the old shepherd who used to tend the flocks for Laius and Jocasta—the man who had passed him the infant child. Oedipus panics. The shepherd denies it. The two men quarrel: "Of course you remember! We were both up there on Mount Cithaeron with the flocks—and you're the person who handed over the baby."

Oedipus senses that things are taking a terrifying turn. For a moment he thinks that perhaps he was merely some foundling, the son of a nymph or a goddess, left exposed on the hillside; that would explain his extraordinary life. He is grasping at a crazy hope, but for the old men gathered there the truth is clear. Oedipus turns to Laius's shepherd and exhorts him to tell the truth.

"Where did you get that child?"

"From this palace."

"Who gave it to you?"

"Jocasta."

There is no longer the shadow of a doubt. Oedipus understands. Like a madman he rushes into the palace to see Jocasta. She has hanged herself by her sash from the ceiling. He finds her already dead. With the brooches from her robe Oedipus slashes his eyes; he bloodies the two orbs.

The legitimate child of a royal and accursed line, thrust out of but then come back to his place of origin—come back not along some normal route, in a straight line, but after digressions and detours—he can see the light no more, he can no longer see anyone's face. He wishes his ears were deaf as well. He wishes he were walled up in utter solitude, for he is become the stain on his city. When there is such a disaster, when the order of the seasons is altered, when fertility is thrown off the straight and normal path, it is because there is a stain, a defilement—and that defilement is himself. He is committed by his promise: He said the murderer would be banished in shame from Thebes: He must go.

MAN: THREE IN ONE

This story makes it quite clear that the Sphinx's riddle foretold the destiny of the House of Labdacus. All animals—two-footed or four, bipeds or quadrupeds, not to mention the footless fishes—have one "nature" that stays the same throughout life. From birth to death there is no change in what defines their particular nature as a living creature. Each species has one condition and only one—one single way of being, one single nature. Man, though, experiences three successive stages, three different natures: First he is an infant, and an infant's nature is different from a full-grown man's. Then, to move from childhood to the adult state, a person must undergo rites of initiation that bring him across the boundaries between the two ages. We become something else, we enter into a new persona when we are no longer child but adult. Similarly—and this is truer still for a king, for a warrior—a person on two feet is *somebody*, with prestige and power that count, but the moment he slips into old age, he ceases to be the man of military prowess; he becomes at best a man of words and of wise counsel, and at worst a pitiable wreck.

Man changes while remaining man throughout these three stages. And Oedipus? The curse leveled on Laius barred births that would continue the Labdacid line. When he was born, Oedipus stepped into the role of a person who ought not to exist. He is out of joint. Laius's child is at once a legitimate descendant and a monstrous offspring. His status is thoroughly crippled. He was meant to die, but he escaped by a miracle. A native of Thebes but straying far from his birthplace, when he happens on to it again and takes up its highest office, he has no idea that he is back at his starting point. So Oedipus's situation is off balance. In journeying back into the palace where he was born, Oedipus has tangled the three stages of human existence. He has overturned the normal sequence of the seasons, mixing the springtime of infancy with the summertime of adulthood and the old man's winter. He has killed his father and at the same time taken on the father's identity by replacing him on the throne and in his mother's bed. Begetting children on his own mother, planting seed in the field that had brought him to life, as the Greeks say, he has shared an identity not only with his father but with his own children, who are both his sons and his brothers, his daughters and his sisters. The monster the Sphinx had described, who is two- and three- and four-footed all at the same time—that monster is Oedipus.

The riddle poses the problem of social continuity—of maintaining status, functions, positions within a culture—despite the flux of generations that are born and reign and die, each giving way to the next. The throne must remain the same while those who occupy it keep changing. How can royal power persist, unitary and intact, when those who exercise it—the kings—are many and diverse? The problem is to know how a king's son can become king like his father, take his place and not clash with him or set him aside, sit on his throne and yet not identify with the father, either, as if he were the same person. How can the flux of the generations, and the sequence of the stages that mark mankind and that are bound up with man's temporal nature, with human imperfection—how can they exist side by side with a social order that must remain stable, coherent, and harmonious? The curse called down on Laius—and perhaps even more, the evil gifts brought to the wedding of Cadmus and Harmonia—are these not a way of acknowledging that into the very core of that extraordinary and foundational marriage there seeped the ferment of disunion, the virus of hatred, as if there were some secret bond between marriage and war, between peace and struggle? There are many—and I am among them—who have said that marriage is the bride and war is the groom. In any city where there are women and men, there is a necessary opposition and a necessary entanglement of combat and marriage.

Oedipus's story does not end there. The House of Labdacus was supposed to stop with Laius, and the curse that weighs on Oedipus reaches far back into the past, well before his birth. He is not to blame, but he does pay the heavy toll that this tribe of cripples, of bunglers, exacts from those who emerged into the light of day when they no longer had the right to be born.

OEDIPUS'S CHILDREN

In Oedipus's blind and sullied state, the story says, his sons treat him so harshly that he in turn casts a curse on his own male offspring, a curse like the one that King Pelops had already laid on Laius. Before he is run out of Thebes, while he is still in the palace, his sons mockingly present the blind man with Cadmus's golden cup and silver table setting, which they then keep for themselves, and they serve Oedipus not a king's rightful portion but the table trash and the offal of sacrificed animals. It is also said that he was locked into a dark cell, to hide him away like a shameful stain to be kept forever secret. So Oedipus casts a solemn curse: that his sons will never settle their differences, that both will seek to wield the royal power, that they will come to armed combat over it and will perish at each other's hands.

And that is what did happen. Those sons, Eteocles and Polynices, descendants of a line that was not supposed to have descendants, conceived a mutual hatred. The two sons agree that they will reign in turn, alternating year by year. Eteocles begins the cycle, but at year's end, he declares that he means to hold onto the throne. Barred from power, Polynices goes off to recruit support in Argos and returns with the expedition of the Seven against Thebes. He attempts to wrest power from his brother by destroying Thebes. In a final battle they kill each other, each his brother's murderer. The House of Labdacus is finished. The story ends there—or seems to.

Polynices' expedition against Thebes was only possible if King

Adrastus of Argos was willing to lead it in support of Polynices' cause. To persuade him, the powerful Argive seer Amphiaraus would have to approve the project. Amphiaraus foresaw, though, that the expedition would be a disaster—that he would die on it and that it would end in a debacle. Therefore he was determined to advise against it. What did Polynices do? As he left Thebes, he took along some of the gifts the gods had given Harmonia when she married Cadmus: a necklace and a robe. He journeyed with these two talismans and presented them as a bribe to Amphiaraus's wife, Eriphyle, so that she would urge her husband to drop his opposition to the expedition against Thebes and urge King Adrastus to do what the seer had heretofore forbidden him to do. Corrupting gifts, malevolent gifts—and gifts that are bound up with a pledge, a vow. Why does the seer yield to his wife? Because he had sworn a vow he can never break: that he would always agree to do what Eriphyle might ask. Evil gifts and irrevocable vows: An element already present at the wedding of Cadmus and Harmonia reappears in the family story, and ends ultimately in the two brothers killing each other.

AN OFFICIAL ALIEN

Oedipus, meanwhile, is hounded from Thebes. Guided by his daughter Antigone, he lives out his life near Colonus, a *deme*, or hamlet, outside Athens. He first stops in forbidden precincts—a sanctuary to the Erinyes, the Furies. The local folk order him to leave: What is this beggar doing in such a holy place? He is as much out of place as was Dionysus turning up in Thebes in his womanish Asian dress. What audacity to try to settle in a place where he cannot even be ejected because no one else may set foot there! The Athenian king Theseus arrives, and Oedipus recounts his misfortunes; he senses that his end is near, and he proposes—if Theseus will take him in—to become the protector of Athens in any conflicts that might arise. Theseus agrees. So this man—this Theban, part of whose heritage is from the warriors born of the Theban soil, but who is also the descendant of Cadmus and Harmonia—is a foreigner here. Ousted from his home at birth, he returned only to be expelled again ignominiously. And now here he is in the last days of his wanderings, without a place, without attachment, without roots—a migrant. Theseus extends him hospitality; he does not make Oedipus a citizen of Athens, but he does accord him the status of *metooikos*, or resident alien—a privileged foreigner. He will live in this land that is not his own and settle here. Oedipus thereby accomplishes a transit to Athens from that divine and accursed Thebes, from that Thebes both united and split apart: a horizontal transit at ground level.

So then: Oedipus becomes an official alien in Athens. It is not the only transition: He also becomes both subterranean—he will be swallowed down into the depths of the earth—and celestial—elevated toward the Olympian gods. He moves from ground level to below ground and again to a position in the heavens. His status is not exactly that of demigod or tutelary hero—a hero's tomb is on the agora, the public square. Instead, at death Oedipus slips into a secret place known only to Theseus, who provides it to persons who govern Athens—a secret tomb that ensures the city's military prowess and its continuity. Here, then, is a foreigner come from Thebes, who establishes a life as an immigrant in Athens, and who dies into the underworld, perhaps struck by a thunderbolt from Zeus. He does not turn into a native born from the local soil as the citizens of Athens claim to be, or into a *gēgēnēs* springing from the Theban earth fully armed and ready for combat. No, he moves in the opposite direction: Arriving as a foreigner, he quits the sunlight to set down roots in the underworld here in this Athenian place that is not his own and to which he brings—in exchange for the hospitality extended him after his sufferings and peregrinations—his pledge of protection through peace and understanding . . . like a faint echo of the promise Harmonia carried, back when the gods gave her as bride to Cadmus, back in that faraway time when Thebes was new.

Perseus, Death, and Image

THE BIRTH OF PERSEUS

Long, long ago, in the good and gracious city of Argos, there lived a powerful king by the name of Acrisius. Even before birth he and his twin brother, Proitus were quarreling in the womb of their mother, Aglaia, punching each other and carrying on a battle that was to last their whole lives. They fought particularly for dominance in that rich Argolis Valley.

Eventually Acrisius ruled over Argos, and Proitus over Tiryns. As king of Argos, Acrisius is heartbroken at having no male child. Following the custom, he goes off to consult the oracle at Delphi to find out whether he is ever to have an heir, and if so, what he must do to bring it about. As usual the oracle does not answer his question, but does indicate that his grandson, his daughter's son, will kill him.

His daughter is called Danaë. She is a very beautiful maiden whom Acrisius loves deeply, but he is terrified at the idea that his grandson is destined to kill him. What can he do? His solution is to lock her away. Indeed, Danaë is fated often to be confined. Acrisius orders the construction—probably in the courtyard of his palace—of a bronze underground prison, and he orders Danaë down into it with a lady-in-waiting; then he carefully locks them both in. Now, from high in the sky, Zeus saw Danaë in the full bloom of her youth and beauty, and he fell in love with her. Men and gods are already living apart, but the distance between them is not yet great enough to prevent the gods, high on Olympus's peak in the shining ether, from occasionally casting a glance down onto the lovely mortal women. They see the daughters of that Pandora whom they sent into the world of men, and to whom Epimetheus had unwisely opened his door; the gods think them splendid. Not that the goddesses aren't beautiful, but the gods may see something in these mortal women that the goddesses lack. It may be the fragility of their beauty, or the fact that they are not immortal and must therefore be plucked when they are still at the peak of their youth and charm.

Zeus falls in love with Danaë, and he smiles at seeing her locked up by her father in that underground bronze prison. Disguised as a golden rain shower, he goes down and slips in beside her—although once inside the prison he may have reshaped his divine person into human appearance. Zeus makes love to Danaë in the utmost secrecy, and Danaë soon bears a child, a boy by the name of Perseus. The whole episode remains clandestine until Perseus, a lusty little fellow, gives forth such yelping that Acrisius, passing through the courtyard one day, hears curious noises from his daughter's prison. The king asks to see her. He has everyone brought up into his presence; he interrogates the nurse and learns that there is a little boy down there. He is seized with terror and fury at once, as he recalls the Delphic oracle. He believes that the servant woman surreptitiously brought someone in to Danaë. He questions his daughter: "Who is this child's father?"

"Zeus."

Acrisius doesn't believe a word of it. He starts by eliminating the servant woman turned nursemaid; in fact he sacrifices her on his household altar to Zeus. But what is he to do with Danaë and the child? A father cannot stain his hands with the blood of his daughter and grandson. He decides to lock them away again.

He calls in a highly skilled, highly talented cabinetmaker, who builds a wooden chest to enclose the pair, Danaë and Perseus. He will entrust the gods with the task of settling this business; this time around he gets rid of them not by imprisonment in his cellars but by throwing open the whole wide ocean to the driftings of his daughter and grandson, sealed into their hiding place. And the chest does float across the sea to the far shores of a modest little island, Seriphos. Dictys, a fisherman (but a fisherman of royal blood), pulls the chest in. He opens it and sees Danaë and her child. He too is enchanted by Danaë's beauty; he brings the young woman and her son to his house; he takes them in as if they were part of his own family. He keeps Danaë with him, treating her with respect, and he raises Perseus like a son: Little Perseus grows up under Dictys's protection.

Dictys's brother, Polydectes, is ruler of Seriphos. Danaë's beauty cuts a swath: King Polydectes in his turn falls wildly in love with her. He is determined to marry her, or at least to win her favors. This is not easy, for Perseus is already nearly full grown, and he keeps close watch over his mother. Dictys is protecting her as well, and Polydectes considers how he should proceed. He decides on the following plan: He arranges a great feast, and invites all the young people of the region. Each is to bring a gift or some contribution to the meal.

THE WAY TO THE GORGONS

King Polydectes presides at the head table. His pretext for the banquet is his supposed intention of marrying a woman called Hippodamia. To win permission to marry her, he must give her guardians luxurious gifts, costly objects. The whole younger generation of Seriphos is present at the banquet, Perseus among them of course. As the meal proceeds the guests all seek to outdo one another in largess and nobility. The king makes a special request for horses: Hippodamia is a passionate rider, he says, and giving her a whole stableful of horses will certainly touch her heart. Perseus wonders what he can do to impress both the other young folk and the king. He declares that he will offer not a mare but anything else the king might want—for instance, the Gorgon's head. He says this without much thought. The next day each young man brings the king the gift he promised; Perseus comes in empty-handed. He offers to give a mare, as the others have, but the king tells him, "No, you bring me the Gorgon's head." And now he cannot do otherwise: If he backs down on his pledge, he will lose face. It is impossible not to keep his promises, or even his boasts. So Perseus is obligated to bring back the Gorgon's head. He is Zeus's son, after all; he has the affection and support of certain deities, especially of Athena and Hermes—clever, cunning, resourceful gods who will see to it that he keeps his promise.

So then: Athena and Hermes help the boy with the feat he must accomplish. They set out the situation for him: The Gorgons are terrifying monsters, sisters who make up a trio of monstrous, death-dealing creatures: Two of them are immortal, but one—Medusa—is mortal. It is Medusa's head he must bring back to the king. To get to the Gorgons he must first learn where they are. And nobody knows where they nest.

The issue, then, is to get to the Gorgons, determine which one is Medusa, and cut off her head. This is no small task. First he must find out where to look for them, and for that Perseus must go through a series of steps, of ordeals, with the help of his protector gods. The first ordeal consists in locating and approaching the Graeae, the "old women"—another three sisters of the Gorgons; all of them are daughters of the very dreadful Phorcus and Ceto, sea monsters as huge as whales. The Graeae dwell in a land not so far off as their sisters; the Gorgons live beyond the Ocean, beyond the borders of the world at the gates of Night, but the Graeae are within the world. Like the Gorgons, they are young maidens, but maidens born old—ancient damsels, young crones. They are deeply wrinkled, shriveled, their skin yellow, like milk left to age that stiffens across its surface and rapidly forms a kind of skin, called *graus*—that wrinkled skin of milk. On the bodies of these maiden deities, instead of a fine white complexion, the monstrosity of a terribly faded, terribly wrinkled old-woman skin. And they have another characteristic: The trio they form is all the tighter, more interdependent, because they share only a single eye and a single tooth among them—as if they were one single self-same creature.

One eye, one tooth: We might think that is not much use, that they are actually at a disadvantage. Not really—for they pass that one eye around among themselves endlessly, so the single eye is forever open and always alert. They have only the single tooth, but these young crones are not so toothless—with that tooth also circulating among them—that they cannot devour all sorts of victims, starting with Perseus.

So—a bit like in the old game of *furet* I used to play as a child—Perseus has got to keep a sharper eye than those three young crones who have only the one but an almost unfailingly vigilant one. He must seize on the moment when their eye is in the hand of none of the three. They keep it moving for constant vigilance, but as one crone passes it to the next there is a brief interval, a short break in the temporal continuity, when Perseus must manage to plunge in, quick as an arrow, and steal the eye. In the *furet* game, several players in a circle hold a cord with a ring strung on it; each player sets his two hands on the cord and passes the ring along from his one hand to the other, and then from that hand to the neighbor's, never letting it show. The person inside the circle is "it," and must guess where the ring is at any moment. If he guesses right, he wins; if he misses, and taps a hand that is hiding nothing, he has lost, and he is penalized.

Perseus doesn't miss—he sees the instant when the eye is in reach, and he seizes it. He captures the tooth as well. The Graeae are in a terrible state, howling with rage and misery. They are blind and toothless now; though immortal, they are reduced to nothing. Obliged to implore Perseus to give them back the eye and the tooth, they will grant him anything in exchange. The one thing he wants from them is the secret of where the nymphs—the *numphai*—live, and how to get there. For the nymphs can show him the way to the Gorgons, and help him with his task.

The word *numphē* describes a girl at the moment when she is just turned nubile, emerged from childhood; she is ready for marriage, good for marrying though not yet a mature woman. These nymphs number three as well. Unlike the Graeae, who spot you and swallow you with their single eye and tooth, the *numphai* are very accessible, welcoming. Perseus has only to ask for what he needs, and they give it to him. They point the way to where the Gorgons hide, and provide him with certain magical items that will allow him to bring off an impossible feat: confronting Medusa's eye and killing the one mortal among the three Gorgons. The nymphs give him winged sandals like those of Hermes, which let the wearer not just advance by one foot after the other on the ground, prosaically, but fly swift as thought, swift as Zeus's eagle, and cross space from south to north with no trouble at all. So: first, speed.

Next the nymphs give him the helmet of Hades—a sort of cap made of dog hide that is also put on the head of a deceased person. Actually the Hades helmet makes the dead faceless, or invisible. That headdress represents the condition of the dead, but if a living person has access to it he too can make himself invisible like a spirit: He can see and not be seen.

Thus: speed and invisibility. They also give him a third gift, a *kybissis*—a beggar's pouch or sack that hunters use to store killed game. Perseus is to deposit Medusa's severed head in the sack so it covers her murderous eyes, like lids closing over them. To all these gifts Hermes adds a personal one—his own *harpē*, the curved sickle that can cut through any obstacle it meets, no matter how hard. Cronus used a *harpē* to castrate Uranus.

Now Perseus is equipped from head to toe: on his feet the sandals, on his head the helmet of invisibility, the *kybissis* hanging on his back and the sickle in his hand. And off he flies toward the three Gorgons.

Who are the Gorgons? They are monstrous beings of utterly contradictory traits; their monstrosity consists in that very condition—incompatible traits in combination. Two of the sisters are partly immortal and the third mortal. They are women, but their heads writhe with hideous serpents, glaring wildly; their shoulders bear enormous golden wings that let them fly like birds; their hands are bronze. Dreadful heads, at once feminine and masculine, despite occasional mention of "beautiful Medusa" or "lovely

Gorgons." Pictures show them with hairy faces. But those whiskery heads are not entirely human, for they also have animal teeth—two long boar tusks jutting from their mouths, which are open in a raw grin with the tongue thrust out. From that twisted mouth comes a kind of fearsome howl, as from a bronze gong that chills you with terror when it's struck.

And the eyes, above all. Their eyes are such that anyone who looks into them turns instantly to stone. The qualities that make for living things—mobility, flexibility, suppleness, warmth, bodily grace—all of that turns to stone. It is not merely a matter of death here—it is the metamorphosis from the human realm to the mineral realm, and thus into what is most antithetic to human nature. It is inescapable. So Perseus's first problem will be to make out which of the three Gorgons he can behead; and then not to meet the glance of any of the three. This means that he will have to cut off Medusa's head without looking her in the face, crossing her field of vision. The gaze plays a powerful role in the Perseus story: With the Graeae he had merely to manage a quicker glance than the monsters to snatch away their eye. But when a person looks at a Gorgon—meets Medusa's gaze—no matter whether one is quick or slow, what one sees reflected in the monster's eyes is oneself turned to stone, oneself become a face out of Hades—a corpse's visage, blind, gazeless.

Perseus would never have succeeded if Athena had not provided advice and an important helping hand. She told him he should land from above, and pick a moment when the two immortal Gorgons were resting, when their eyes were closed. As to Medusa, he must behead her without ever meeting her gaze. To do so he will have to turn his own head aside at the very instant of wielding the *harpē*. But if he looks aside, how will he see the way to cut off her head? Unless he looks, he will not know her position, and he risks slicing off an arm or some other part of her body. So, as with the Graeae, he has to know exactly where to land the blow, confirm it by one precise, unerring glance—and at the same time avoid sighting his target's petrifying eye.

A great paradox. Athena solves the problem: He should set the goddess's fine polished shield before the Gorgon at such an angle that, without meeting Medusa's gaze, Perseus can see her reflection in the mirroring armor clearly enough to tailor his gesture and slice through her neck as if he were seeing her directly. He severs her head, catches it as it falls, and thrusts it into the *kybissis*. He buckles up the sack and darts away.

The two other Gorgons wake up at Medusa's scream. With the strident, hideous howls they are known for, they hurl themselves after Perseus. Like them, he can take to the air; but he has the further advantage of being invisible. They try to catch up to him; he escapes them; they are beside themselves with rage.

ANDROMEDA'S BEAUTY

Perseus reaches the eastern shores of the Mediterranean, in Ethiop. As he flies through the air, he sees a very beautiful young woman bolted to a rock, with the waves washing her feet. The sight moves him. This young person is Andromeda; she was put in that sorry position by her father, King Cepheus. His land is assailed by terrible plagues; the king and his people have been told that the only way to end the scourge is to hand over Andromeda to a sea monster—a creature linked to the sea, to the waters that can drown the land—and to expose her there so that the beast can come take her and have his will of her: devour her or couple with her.

The poor girl moans, her cry rises up to Perseus as he hovers on the breeze above; he hears her, he sees her. His heart is won over by Andromeda's beauty. He goes to find Cepheus, who explains. Perseus pledges to free his daughter from her fate if he may have her as his bride. The father accepts, thinking that in any event the young man will never succeed. Perseus returns to where Andromeda stands shackled on her little rock amid the waves. The monster is moving toward her—immense, formidable, and apparently invincible. What can Perseus do? With its maw gaping wide, its tail lashing the waves, the monster closes in on the lovely Andromeda. High in the air, Perseus positions himself between the sun and the sea so that his shadow falls onto the waters directly in front of the beast's eyes—the shadow caught on the mirror of the waters, as Medusa's reflection was caught on Athena's shield: Perseus has not forgotten the lesson the goddess taught him. Seeing the shadow darting before it, the monster imagines that this is the thing that is threatening him. He lunges for the shadow—and Perseus drops onto him from the sky above and kills him.

Perseus kills the monster and then releases Andromeda. He takes her to the shore—, and makes what might be a mistake. Andromeda is deeply agitated; distraught, she tries to recover a little life and hope again there on the beach, amid the boulders. Meaning to free his movements so he might comfort her, Perseus sets down his heavy sack on the sand—and its edge pulls back slightly to expose Medusa's eyes. The Gorgon's gaze stretches out across the waters; the algae floating there, all supple, mobile, and alive, turn solid, petrified, transformed into blood-red corals. This is how there came to be mineralized algae in the sea: Medusa's gaze changed them to stone amid the waves.

Perseus then carries Andromeda away with him. He shoulders his tightly locked sack and he reaches Seriphos, where his mother awaits him. Dictys is waiting too. The two have taken refuge in a sanctuary to escape Polydectes. Perseus decides to take revenge on the evil king. He lets him know he is back, and that he has the promised gift; he will present it to him at a banquet. All the island's youths and men are gathered in the great hall, and everyone is drinking and eating—very festive. Perseus arrives. He opens the door, he is greeted, he enters—and Polydectes wonders what is about to happen.

All the guests are sitting or reclining, but Perseus is still standing. He reaches into his sack for the Medusa head; he lifts it out, and, looking away toward the door, he brandishes it at arm's length. The banqueters freeze in their various positions: Some are drinking, others talking, their mouths are open, their eyes turned to watch Perseus come into the hall. The revelers are transformed into tableaux, into statues. They become mute and blind images, reflections of what they were alive. Perseus opens the sack and puts back the head with its petrifying eye. He seems to have finished with the Medusa affair.

There is still the grandfather, Acrisius. Perseus knows that Acrisius treated him as he did because he believed that his grandson was destined to bring about his death. The young man thinks some peace might be possible with his forefather, so he leaves for Argos with Andromeda, Danaë, and Dictys. But the terrified Acrisius—aware that the child Perseus is now a grown man, that he has accomplished great things, and that he is heading for Argos—has gone to a neighboring town.

When Perseus reaches Argos, he is told that Acrisius has left town to take part in some games. Among them is a contest of discus hurling. Young Perseus arrives and is invited to join in—he is handsome, well built, and in his prime. He takes up his discus and hurls it. By utter chance the discus lands on Acrisius's foot, and causes a mortal wound. With the king dead, the throne of Argos comes to Perseus, but he hesitates about taking it: It seems a bad idea to succeed a king whose death he has caused. He works out a kind of family reconciliation by means of an exchange: Proitus, the dead king's brother, is ruler of Tiryns, so he proposes that Proitus should move to the Argos throne, and he—Perseus—will take his place in Tiryns.

First, though, he gives back the tools of his victory over Medusa to those who had lent them. He returns Hermes' *harpē* and asks the messenger to carry the winged sandals, the sack, and the helmet of Hades beyond the human world to their legitimate owners, the nymphs. The Gorgon's severed head he offers in thanks to Athena, who makes it the central ornament of her armor. Displayed on the battlefield, the goddess's Gorgoneion shield paralyzes the enemy where he stands, frozen with terror, and sends him off—transformed into a phantom, a spectral double, an *eidolon*—to the land of the shades, in Hades.

A mere mortal again now, the hero Perseus—whose feats had long made him a "master of death"—eventually dies in turn like anyone else. But to honor the young man who dared to brave the Gorgon with the petrifying gaze, Zeus transports Perseus to heaven; he sets him out in the constellation that bears his name and that traces his figure on the dark nighttime vault in points of light that all the world can see, forevermore.

Glossary

Achilles   Son of Thetis and Peleus. The greatest hero of the Trojan War. Preferred the undying glory of premature death to peaceful but obscure longevity.

Acrisius   King of Argos, father of Danaë. Killed by his hero grandson, Perseus, on the latter's return from killing Medusa.

Adrastus   King of Argos and father-in-law of Oedipus's son Polynices, who, driven from Thebes by his brother, leads the expedition known as the Seven against Thebes.

Aegipan   Helps Hermes retrieve Zeus's severed sinews.

Aegisthus   Son of Thyestes, enemy of the House of Atreus. Seduces Queen Clytemnestra and, with her assistance, kills her husband, Agamemnon, on his triumphal return from Troy.

Aeneas   Son of Anchises and Aphrodite, and a fighter for Troy. After the city's fall, manages to escape carrying his aged father on his back; eventually reaches southern Italy.

Aeolus   Ruler of the winds. Welcomes Odysseus to his island and gives him a goatskin confining all the winds but the one that will blow him straight home to Ithaca.

Aether   Son of Night; personifies the pure and constant celestial light.

Agamemnon   King of Argos. Leader of the Greeks during the Trojan War; at its end, murdered by his wife, Clytemnestra.

Agave   Daughter of Cadmus and mother of Pentheus.

Agenor   King of Tyre or Sidon; father of Europa.

Aglaia   One of the Charites (the Graces).

Alcinous   King of the Phaeacians, husband of Arete, and father of Nausicaa. Offers Odysseus hospitality and a ship to take him back to Ithaca.

Alexander Other name of Paris, Helen's seducer; son of Priam.

Amphiaraus Argive seer, husband of Eriphyle. Approved the Seven against Thebes expedition, during which he met his death.

Amphion Son of Zeus and Antiope; kills Lycus, the king of Thebes, and along with his brother, Zethus, takes his place.

Amphitrite A nereid, wife of Poseidon.

Anchises Trojan. Couples with Aphrodite on Mount Ida; their child is Aeneas.

Andromeda Daughter of Cepheus, king of the Ethiops. To propitiate Poseidon, he bolts her to a rock as an offering to a sea monster. She is rescued by Perseus.

Antigone Daughter of Oedipus. Accompanies her blind father into exile.

Antinous One of Penelope's suitors.

Aphrodite Goddess of love, seduction, and beauty; born of the sea and the foamy sperm of castrated Uranus. Paris awards her the golden apple as the most beautiful of the goddesses.

Ares God of war.

Arges One of the three Cyclops—sons of Uranus and Gaia.

Argus   Odysseus's dog. Nothing escaped him; he had his eye on everything.

Artemis   Daughter of Zeus and Leto, sister of Apollo. Hunter-goddess who fights beside the Olympians against the Titans.

Athamas   Boeotian king. His second wife is Ino, a daughter of Cadmus.

Athena   Daughter of Zeus and Metis; springs fully armed from her father's head. Goddess of war and intelligence. Competes with Hera and Aphrodite in the judgment of Paris.

Atlas   Son of the Titan Iapetus and brother of Prometheus. Zeus condemns him to support heaven's vault on his back.

Autolycus   Son of Hermes, grandfather of Odysseus. Liar, thief.

Autonoë   A daughter of Cadmus. Mother of Acteon, who is torn apart by his own dogs.

Balius   One of Achilles' horses. Immortal and capable of speech. (See *Zanthus*.)

Bellerophon Corinthian hero; kills the Chimera with the help of the horse Pegasus.

Bie   Daughter of Styx. Personifies the ruler's violence.

Boreus   North wind.

Briareus   One of the three Hundred-Armed Giants, the
                  Hecatonchires, who are brothers of the Cyclopes and
                  the Titans, all offspring of Uranus and Gaia.

Brontes   One of the three Cyclops—sons of Uranus and Gaia.

Cadmus   Son of Agenor, king of Sidon. With his mother,
                  Telephassa, goes off in search of his sister, Europa.
                  Husband of Harmonia; founder and first king of
                  Thebes.

Calydon   Region of Aetolia north of the Gulf of Corinth.

Castor   One of the Dioscuri, son of Zeus and Leda; a horseman,
                  and expert in the art of war. Unlike his brother, Pollux,
                  he is mortal.

Centaurs   Monsters with human heads and chests, horselike
                  bodies; live wild in forests and mountains, but can
                  also train young Greek heroes.

Cepheus   King of the Ethiops and father of Andromeda.

Cerberus   Dog of Hades. Guards kingdom of the dead, keeping
                  the living from entering and the deceased from
                  leaving.

Ceto   Sea monster, daughter of Pontus and Gaia, and
                  mother of the Graeae and the Gorgons.

Chaos   Void; primordial element from which the world
                  emerges.

Charybdis   Sea monster/whirlpool, who from her rock swallows all passing ships. (See *Scylla*.)

Chimera   Flame-breathing creature with three heads (goat, lion, snake). Born of Echidna and the monster Typhon.

Chiron   Very wise and benign Centaur, living on Mount Pelion. Teacher of heroes, Achilles in particular.

Chrysippe   Young son of King Pelops of Corinth. The boy is courted by Laius, his father's guest, who tries to take him by force, provoking his suicide.

Chthonius   One of the five survivors of the battle among the Spartoi—the "sown men" born of dragon's teeth from the soil of Thebes.

Cicones   A people of Thrace, allies of the Trojans. Sailing back from the war, Odysseus lands there and plunders their city, Ismaros. But then the Greeks are attacked from all sides and must take to the sea again and flee.

Cilix   Son of Agenor, king of Sidon. Like his brother, Cadmus, and his mother, Telephassa, he goes in search of his sister, Europa.

Cimmerians   People living near the gates of Hades, in a region where the sun never shines.

Circe   Sorceress, and a daughter of the sun, she lives on the island of Aeaea. Turns Odysseus's companions into pigs. Bested by the hero, she becomes his lover, and they live a long while together.

Clytemnestra   Daughter of Zeus and Leda, Helen's sister, and wife of Agamemnon, whom she cuckolds with Aegisthus and murders on his return from Troy.

Cottus   One of the three Hundred-Armed Creatures, the Hecatonchires.

Creon   Jocasta's brother. Regent of Thebes between the death of Laius and the arrival of Oedipus.

Cronus   Youngest of the Titans, first sovereign of the world.

Cyclopes   Ogre sons of Uranus and Gaia, each with a single eye flashing in the middle of his forehead: Brontes, Steropes, Arges. Another, Polyphemus, is a son of Poseidon.

Danaë   Daughter of Acrisius; mother of Perseus after secretly receiving Zeus as a golden shower in the underground chamber where her father, Acrisius, imprisoned her.

Deiphobus   Son of Priam and Hecuba. Brother of Hector. Plays a role in the early negotiations between the Greeks and the Trojans. Killed by Menelaus in the siege of the city.

Dictys   Brother of King Polydectes of Seriphos. Rescues and protects Danaë and Perseus after their banishment by Acrisius.

Dionysus   Son of Zeus and Semele. Returns to his birthplace, Thebes, to establish his cult.

Dioscuri   Castor and Pollux, the twin sons of Zeus and Tyndareus's wife, Leda. They are brothers of Helen and Clytemnestra.

Echidna   Half woman, half snake. Coupling with Typhon, she bears a whole series of monsters.

Echion   One of the five Spartoi; husband of Agave, father of Pentheus.

Eos   Dawn. Goddess who falls in love with the human Tithonus and persuades Zeus to grant him immortality.

Epimetheus   Brother of Prometheus, and his opposite. Instead of knowing things beforehand, he only understands them too late, afterward. Takes Pandora into his household and marries her.

Erebus   Son of Chaos. Personifies darkness.

Erinyes   The Furies, avenger goddesses, born of the blood from Uranus's castration.

Eriphyle   Wife of Amphiaraus. Bribing her with Harmonia's necklace, Polynices wins her support for his war against Thebes, where his brother Eteocles reigns.

Eros   God of love. (1) The old Eros: one of the three original divinities; (2) Eros, son of Aphrodite: presides over sexual bonding, sexual relations.

Eteocles   Son of Oedipus. Rival of his brother, Polynices, he refuses to share the throne of Thebes after their father's departure.

Eumaeus   Odysseus's swineherd, ever faithful to his master.

Europa   Daughter of Agenor, king of Tyre or Sidon. Carried off to Crete by Zeus in the guise of a bull.

Eurycleia   Odysseus's old nurse; she is one of the first to recognize him as she washes his feet and sees the scar on his leg.

Eurylochus   Companion and brother-in-law of Odysseus. His initiatives and advice are not of the best.

Gaia   The Earth as a deity.

Giants   Born of the drops of blood from Uranus's castration. Personifications of battle and war.

Gorgons   Three monsters whose glance kills. Only one of them, Medusa, is mortal, and Perseus beheads her.

Graeae   Three aged maidens who share a single tooth and eye. Perseus seizes both from them.

Gyes   One of the three Hundred-Armed Creatures, the Hecatonchires.

Hades   A son of Cronus and Rhea, like all the Olympians.
               God of death, who reigns over the underworld of the
               shades.

Harmonia   Daughter of Ares and Aphrodite. Wife of Cadmus.

Harpies   Monsters with the body of a bird and the head of a
               woman. They attack humans and carry them off
               without a trace.

Hecate   Daughter of Titans, this moon goddess is particularly
               honored by Zeus.

Hecuba   Wife of Priam, king of Troy. Mother of Hector.

Hecaton-   Hundred-Armed Creatures; trio of Gaia and
chires   Uranus's offspring: Cottus, Briareus, Gyes.
               Invincibly powerful giants each with fifty heads
               and a hundred arms.

Helios   The sun god.

Hemere   Daughter of Night. Personifies daylight.

Hephaestus Son of Zeus and Hera. Patron of metalworking.

Hera   Zeus's wife.

Heracles   The hero of the twelve labors. His human parents are
               Amphitryon and Alcmene, descendants of Perseus; his
               true father is Zeus.

Hermes	Son of Zeus and the nymph Maia, this youthful messenger god is associated with motion, contacts, transactions, crossings, commerce. He links the earth and sky, the living and dead.
Hesiod	Boeotian poet, author of the *Theogony* and *Works and Days*.
Hestia	Goddess of the home. She is the last of his children swallowed by Cronus, and the first to reappear (after the stone) when he is made to vomit them up.
Himeros	Personification of erotic desire.
Hippodamia	Daughter of Oenomaus, king of Elide, who demanded that to win her hand, suitors must best him in a chariot race.
Homer	Author of *The Iliad* and *The Odyssey*.
Horai	The Hours: three daughters of Zeus and Thetis, sisters of the Moirai. Divinities of the seasons, which they regulate.
Hyperenor	One of the five Spartoi.
Hypnos	Personification of sleep. Son of Night and Erebus, and brother of Thanatos—Death.
Iapetus	One of the Titans; father of Prometheus.

Idas   Brother of Lynceus and cousin of the Dioscuri. In a battle Idas kills Castor and wounds Pollux. Zeus blasts him with lightning to help his son Pollux.

Idomeneus   Chief of the Cretan contingent in the Trojan War. One of Helen's suitors.

Ino   Daughter of Cadmus and Harmonia, and aunt of Dionysus. Marries Athamas and persuades him to take in the young Dionysus. Jealous Hera renders the couple mad; Ino throws herself into the water and becomes the nereid Leucothea.

Irus   Established beggar at Penelope's palace in Ithaca. Odysseus punishes him for trying to keep him out.

Ismaros   Thracian city, in the land of the Cicones. On his way home Odysseus seizes it but is then driven away by the peasants of the area.

Ismene   Daughter of Oedipus and sister of Antigone.

Jocasta   Wife of Laius and mother of Oedipus, whom she unwittingly marries.

Keres   Daughters of Night—forces of death and disaster.

Kratus   Son of Styx. Personifies the power of sovereign domination. (See *Bie*.)

Labdacids   The House of Labdacus, on which Pelops casts a curse.

Labdacus   Grandson of Cadmus, and on his mother's side, of the "sown man" Chthonius. Father of Laius and grandfather of Oedipus.

Laertes   Father of Odysseus.

Laius   King of Thebes, son of Labdacus, father of Oedipus, and husband of Jocasta.

Leda   Daughter of Thestius, king of Calydon. Wife of Tyndareus. In the guise of a swan, Zeus couples with her. Mother of Helen, Clytemnestra, Castor, and Pollux.

Laestry-   Man-eating Giants.
gonians

Leucothea   Ino's name after her transformation into a benevolent divinity and rescuer of the shipwrecked.

Limos   Personification of hunger.

Lotophagi   The lotus eaters, who lose their memory as a result.

Lycurgus   King of Thrace. Pursues the young Dionysus, who leaps into the ocean to escape him.

Lycus   Brother of Nicteus and son of the "sown man" Chthonius.

Lynceus   Brother of Idas. Famed for his piercing gaze. Killed by Pollux during the battle in which he and his brother fight their cousins, the Dioscuri.

Maron   Priest of Apollo in Ismaros, whom Odysseus spares
               during the destruction of the city. Gives the Greek
               hero a wonder-working wine.

Mecone   Marvelously fertile plain near Corinth.

Medea   Daughter of Aeëtes, king of Colchis;
               granddaughter of the Sun and Circe's niece; sorceress.

Medusa   The mortal one of the three Gorgons; Perseus
               beheads her.

Meliai   Bellicose ash-tree nymphs.

Menelaus   King of Argos, brother of Agamemnon, and
               husband of Helen.

Metis   First wife of Zeus and mother of Athena. Personifies
               cunning intelligence.

Minos   King of Crete. Judge in Hades.

Moirae   The three Fates, who preside over the assignment of
               destinies.

Muses   Singing divinities; the nine daughters of Zeus and
               Mnemosyne (Memory).

Nausicaa   Daughter of the king and queen of Phaeacia.
               Encounters Odysseus and gives him advice and
               guidance, aiming to have him received as a guest by
               her parents. She thinks he would make a very good
               husband.

Nemesis   Goddess of retribution. Daughter of Night. Zeus couples with her against her will, she in the guise of a goose, he of a swan. She lays an egg that Leda is sent as a gift.

Nereids   The fifty daughters of Nereus, god of the sea, and of Doris, a daughter of Oceanus. They live in their father's palace at the bottom of the sea, but also sometimes appear playing in the waves.

Nereus   Son of Gaia and Pontus. God known as the Old Man of the Sea.

Nestor   The oldest of the Greek combatants in the Trojan War. A man of garrulous wisdom, he talks readily and nostalgically of his long-ago exploits.

Nicteis   Daughter of the "sown man" Chthonius. Wife of Polydorus and mother of Labdacus.

Nicteus   Son of the "sown man" Chthonius. Brother of Lycos.

Notos   The hot and humid south wind.

Nux   Night, daughter of Chaos.

Nymphs (Numphai)   Daughters of Zeus, youthful minor goddesses of the springs, rivers, woods, and countrysides.

Oedipus   Son of Laius and Jocasta. Exposed at birth because an oracle foretold that he would kill his father and sleep with his mother—which he unwittingly does.

Oceanus   Ocean. One of the Titans. River encircling the world.

Odysseus   King of Ithaca.

Olympus   Mountain on whose summit the Olympian gods dwell.

Othrys   Mountain to which the Titans withdraw to fight the Olympians.

Oudaius   One of the five "sown men."

Pan   God of herds and shepherds; son of Hermes.

Pandora   The first woman, a gift from the Olympian gods to Epimetheus, who accepts it despite his brother Prometheus's warning.

Paris   Youngest son of King Priam and Queen Hecuba of Troy; also known as Alexander. Exposed at birth, later recognized by his parents. Abducts and marries Helen.

Pegasus   Divine (winged) horse that emerges from Medusa's severed neck and flies to Olympus. Carries Zeus's thunder.

Peleus   King of Phthia and husband of Thetis. Father of Achilles.

Pelion   Mountain in Thessaly where Peleus and Thetis's wedding is celebrated and where the centaur Chiron instructs Achilles as a hero.

Pelops Son of Tantalus and husband of Hippodamia. Father of Chrysippe, who commits suicide to avoid the attentions of Laius. Pelops casts a curse on Laius's line, the Labdacids.

Pelorus One of the "sown men."

Pentheus Grandson of Cadmus on his mother's, Agave's, side, and son of Echion, a "sown man." Opposes Dionysus when the god returns to Thebes.

Periboea Wife of Polybius, the king of Corinth; they adopt the infant Oedipus, who had been exposed at birth by his parents.

Perseus Son of Zeus and Danaë. Thrown into the sea with his mother by his grandfather, Acrisius, and beached on the island of Seriphos, he is enjoined by the island's king to bring him Medusa's head.

Phaeacians Seafaring people. Toward the end of his voyage they carry Odysseus from the other world to the human world, and deposit him, asleep, on a beach in Ithaca.

Philoetius Odysseus's old cowherd, still faithful to his master.

Phoenix One of Agenor's sons. Like his brothers, goes in search of Europa after her abduction by Zeus.

Phorcus Son of Gaia and Pontus. His union with Ceto produces the three Graeae and the Gorgons.

Pollux   Brother of Castor (see *Dioscuri*). Expert boxer. Immortal from birth, he determines to share his immortality with his brother.

Polybius   King of Corinth. Oedipus's pseudofather.

Polydectes   King of Seriphos. In love with Danaë. Sends Perseus off to bring him Medusa's head.

Polydorus   Son of Cadmus and Harmonia. Husband of Nicteis, daughter of the "sown man" Chthonius, and father of Labdacus.

Polynices   Son of Oedipus, brother of Eteocles. The rivalry between the two leads to their confrontation and deaths.

Polyphemus   Cyclops son of Poseidon. Duped and blinded by Odysseus, he takes vengeance by casting a highly effective curse on the hero.

Pontus   Sea as deity; born of Gaia.

Poseidon   Olympian god, brother of Zeus. Rules over the ocean waters.

Priam   King of Troy, husband of Hecuba, and father of Hector and Paris.

Proitus   Twin brother and rival of Acrisius. Reigns in Tyrins.

Prometheus   Son of the Titan Iapetus. Benefactor to humans, in conflict with Zeus.

Proteus   Sea god, endowed with the power of metamorphosis and the gift of prophecy.

Rhada-   Son of Zeus and Europa. Brother of Minos, the ruler
manthus   of Crete. For his wisdom he is charged with judging the dead in Hades.

Rhea   Titan daughter of Uranus and Gaia; sister and wife of Cronus.

Satyrs   Creatures that are top half man, bottom half either horse or goat, usually with erection. They are part of Dionysus's retinue.

Scylla   Monster who lies in wait for and devours the crews of the ships that pass between him and the whirlpool, Charybdis.

Semele   Daughter of Cadmus and Harmonia. Loved by Zeus. She is consumed in the blaze of her divine lover while she is pregnant with Dionysus.

Sphinx   Female monster with the head and breasts of a woman and the body of a winged lion. Puts to death those who cannot solve her riddle, which Oedipus unravels.

Steropes   A Cyclops, one of the sons of Uranus and Gaia.

Styx   Elder daughter of Oceanus; personifies the infernal river that separates the living from the dead.

Talos   Metallic watchman of Crete.

Tartarus   Gloomy underworld, where defeated gods and the
dead are shut away. Also, the lord of that place.

Telemachus   Son of Odysseus and Penelope.

Telephassa   Wife of Agenor and mother of Cadmus and
Europa.

Thasus   Son of Agenor and brother of Cadmus.

Theseus   Hero of Attica and king of Athens. His mother is
Aethra, his human father Egeus, his divine father
Poseidon.

Thestius   Father of Leda.

Thetis   One of the nereids; wife of Peleus and mother of
Achilles.

Tiresias   Seer inspired by Apollo. He alone recognizes Oedipus
when the hero returns to his native Thebes.

Titan   Children of Uranus and Gaia (Heaven and Earth).
Gods of the first generation, who battle the
Olympians for sovereignty of the universe.

Tithonus   Brother of Priam. The goddess Eos loves him for his
beauty. She abducts him and persuades Zeus to grant
him immortality.

Tyndareus   Leda's husband; father of the Dioscuri, of Helen,
and of Clytemnestra.

Typhon	Or Typheus. Monster son of Gaia and Tartarus. Struggles with Zeus, who finally vanquishes him.
Uranus	The Sky as divinity; born of Gaia.
Zanthus	Achilles' horse; immortal, and capable of speech when necessary.
Zephyr	Gentle, steady wind.
Zethus	Son of Zeus and Antiope. Along with his brother, Amphion, kills Lycus so as to avenge his mother, a victim of ill treatment at the hands of Lycus and his wife. Thereafter ascends the throne of Thebes.
Zeus	Olympian, sovereign of the gods; conqueror of the Titans and of the monsters threatening the cosmic order he established as sovereign of the universe.